A Rumour
of
Adventure

An Inklings Story

Kees M. Paling

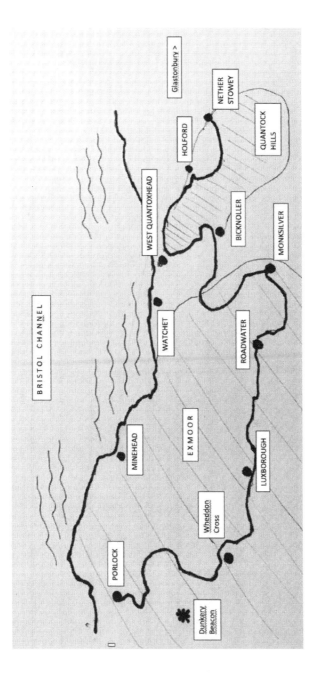

DEDICATION

I dedicate this book to my brother Michiel Paling,
who is always willing to read my stories and who listens
patiently to all my crazy ideas for yet another book.

CONTENTS

ACKNOWLEDGMENTS

I owe much to the wonderful literature about the
Inklings and the individual members of the group.
And although this book is fiction, I have added a list of
the literature I used.
I owe even more to my family and friends who were
willing to read a chapter as soon as I had finished it.
Their comments on structure and the use of the English
language were very helpful.

AN UNEXPECTED JOURNEY

Oxford, March 1938

It was a bleak Tuesday morning and Professor Tolkien had just finished his lectures at Pembroke College. As a professor of Anglo-Saxon with a special interest in Philology he had discussed some 'very fascinating' aspects of medieval English. Despite his quotations from Norse and Icelandic sagas, the lecture had not been very interesting. How different would it have been, had he told his students about the lives of dragons, like he did last January in the University of Oxford Museum for a bunch of kids. At the age of 46 and having been a professor since 1925, Tolkien had developed a special and lifelong interest in the world of faerie. A world inhabited by giants, goblins, elves and dwarfs, ruled by the principles of magic and fantasy.

What once started as a kind of philological hobby - the construction of Elfin languages akin to the grammar and vocabulary of Welsh and Finnish - had resulted in the creation of a complete imaginary world, called 'Middle Earth'. The history of this world was described in many different but interrelated sagas, spanning several eras in time.

Last year saw the publication of *The Hobbit.* This 'children's book' tells the story of the hobbit Bilbo Baggins, who stumbles upon an adventure with dwarfs in search of their long lost treasure, guarded by a dragon. Although hobbits are very different from men and even smaller than dwarfs, an independent observer would also note some peculiar similarities between the hobbits of Middle Earth and this special breed of men called 'the Oxford dons'. Like hobbits these Oxfordonians wear uniform clothing - tweed jackets, baggy (Baggins?) trousers - they love to eat and drink all day; talk a lot about important topics like the weather today, yesterday and tomorrow; but most of all they dislike adventures and anything else that might disrupt their daily routine.

After leaving the monumental buildings of Pembroke College, Tolkien walked up to St. Aldate's from where he had a good view of the 'Tom Gate', the entrance to Christ Church on the other side of the road. Towering above the gate was the old bell tower that housed 'Great Tom', maybe not the biggest, but certainly the loudest bell of all Oxford. It was installed in the 17th century during the reign of Charles II and ever since chimes 101 times every night at 21.00 hours old Oxford time (which is about five minutes later than GMT).

That morning Tolkien had no time to admire the old structures and continued on his way along St. Aldate's in the direction of Cornmarket and St. Giles'. As on every Tuesday morning, he was about to meet some of his friends at 'The Eagle and Child', a local pub which they frequented every week for a drink, some food and a bit of small talk. The tradition originated somewhere in the 1920's with regular meetings of Oxford dons to discuss literary matters. They called themselves 'The Inklings', but even that name was 'inherited' from one of the earlier groups. Nowadays they gathered twice a week: on Tuesday mornings in the local pub and on Thursday evenings in C.S. Lewis' rooms at Magdalen College. The membership of 'The Inklings' changed over time and in fact never had an official determination. The nucleus of the group was formed by Tolkien and 'Jack' Lewis. Other more or less regular members were Jack's older brother Warnie, Hugo Dyson, Owen Barfield, Charles Williams, Neville Coghill and Robert Havard. On Thursday evenings they read each other the first drafts of essays, novels and fairy stories, and there was time for debate and criticism. Over a pint of beer Tolkien had shared with them the adventures of Bilbo Baggins and recently he had started to read them the first chapters of 'The New Hobbit'. It was the sequel that his publisher had asked him to write, but it would still take quite some years before it would be finished.

Walking along St. Aldate's and Cornmarket and crossing Queen Street, Tolkien passed the Oxford Town Hall with its ornamental entrance. The Gothic character was misleading, because in years Tolkien was in fact older than the building. A genuine old structure, however, was 'St. Michael at the North Gate', the building at the next crossing, just before entering Magdalen street. The church was called this way, because it was the location of the original North Gate when Oxford was still surrounded by a city wall. With a Saxon tower which was erected in 1040, the church was by far the oldest building in Oxford.

After he passed the tower and walked through Magdalen Street, Tolkien entered St. Giles', from where it would take him only a few minutes to reach the 'Eagle and Child'. Tolkien walked on the left side of the street, with firm steps, though not very fast. He liked to look around during his walks, pay attention to buildings and ornaments and observe the people and the traffic in the city. It was this same tendency that sometimes brought his friends to despair. During walking tours Tolkien would slow down his companions while he stood still to observe the flowers in the field and the birds in the trees. He would comment on their type, color and variation, with the knowledge of an expert, but without realising that he was delaying the whole tour. As one of his friends once remarked: 'he's reducing our walking tour to some kind of Sunday stroll'.

Upon reaching 'The Eagle and Child' (they nicknamed it 'The Bird and Baby'), Tolkien glanced at the familiar sign outside the pub. It depicted a large eagle, ready to fly, with a child on it's back a child; the child - no more than a baby - clad in just a loincloth. It was supposed to be a representation of the Greek myth of Jove, abducting the little prince Ganymede. Why the owner of the pub ever picked this scene for the name of his tavern no one really knew. At the same time the mythological scene may have inspired Tolkien when he was writing 'The Hobbit', as in the book the hobbit Bilbo Baggins and his company of dwarfs are saved by a flock of eagles from an assault by malicious wargs and orcs.

Tolkien entered the pub, said 'good morning' to the locals inside and then walked on to the more private room in the back, called 'The Rabbit Room'. It was a large, rectangular room with dark paneling along the walls. The room was dimly lit and the air was filled with smoke. At the table in front of the wooden fireplace Tolkien found two regulars of 'The Inklings' already present, both puffing smoke from the pipes in their hands.

'Hwaet, we Inclinga!!' Tolkien shouted, lifting his arms as if trying to embrace both his friends. One of them, Jack (C.S.) Lewis, laughed at this theatrical gesture and welcomed him: 'Morning, Tollers, come and join us.' Tolkien shook hands with Owen Barfield, the other person at the table, and then took a seat next to Lewis. For some time Barfield had been a regular at their meetings until a few years ago, when for purely financial reasons he moved to London to become a solicitor at his father's office. Tolkien was surprised to see him.

'Well, Barfield', he started, 'how nice to see you after quite some time. What brings you to Oxford this morning?'

Barfield smiled and said: 'nothing in particular, actually. I guess it was a yearning for old times.'

'It's a big mistake!', Lewis interrupted, 'he really thinks we have all the fun up here.'

Tolkien laughed and stuffed some tobacco in his pipe. He lit a match and within a minute he was producing impressive puffs of smoke.

Barfield shook his head. 'No', he said, 'I know the troubles of Oxford college life well enough from your stories. But believe me, it's far more exciting than the life of a barrister in London.'

'Ah!' Lewis said, raising his forefinger, 'so that's it: no Sherlock Holmes stories or Jack the Ripper, just the average cases of adultery, fraud and missing doggies?'

'Oh no,' Barfield replied, again shaking his head, 'not at all! You confuse the work of a barrister with that of a private detective. For me missing doggies would be an adventure! Instead, I am occupied with a lot of boring files and paperwork for most of the day.'

'I'm sorry to hear that, Barfield', Tolkien said, between two puffs, 'I do hope you still have time for reflection and perhaps some writing'.

Well, yes', Barfield replied with a wave of his hand, 'don't misunderstand me, I shan't complain and of course it pays the rent, but sometimes it can become quite boring'.

At that moment another member of the Inklings entered the room. It was Charles Williams, editor of the Oxford University Press, which was established in London.

'Charles!' Lewis exclaimed, 'what a surprise! Aren't you supposed to be in London?'

'Well, yes, of course', Charles answered, taking a seat next to Barfield, 'but fortunately our publishing company sometimes wishes to remain in contact with the authors in Oxford.' He smiled when he continued: 'and as you are all in a way authors, I thought this would be a good way to spend the morning.' They all laughed and Lewis waved to the barman to bring them some drinks.

Soon there was ale and cider on the table and each gentleman took a sip of his favorite drink.

Williams lit a cigarette and joined in the smoke-puffing around the table.

'Have you heard?' he said after blowing out some smoke, 'right at this moment Mr. Hitler seems to be publicly addressing the people of Vienna.' Two days earlier the Germans had invaded Austria and called it 'Anschluss'.

Tolkien grumbled and Lewis said: 'I'm sure he will.' And with a disdain in his voice he added: 'And I can guess what the message will be: there is no such thing as an occupation of Austria, only the liberation of another German-speaking people. Who can oppose that?'

Barfield sighed. 'I just hope it ends there. What more can he want?'

Tolkien shook his head and said: 'I don't know what he wants, but this man is evil. I'm afraid he won' t stop there.'

'Really?' Lewis asked, 'do you know what you are saying, Tollers?'

'Yes, of course', Tolkien answered, 'I just hope I'm wrong. I guess we've had enough war in our lifetime.' The others muttered in agreement.

For a few moments they drank and smoked in silence. Lewis broke the spell by introducing a much happier topic: 'By the way, we haven't yet made plans for a walking tour this spring.'

7

Every year a number of the Inklings made a walking tour together, usually for a few days.

'True', Williams confirmed, 'you're quite right. Any suggestions? Where shall we go this year?'

Puffing their pipes they reflected on the possibilities.

'How about the Cotswolds?' Barfield tried.

'Mhhh', Lewis reacted, without much enthusiasm, 'I was there last year.'

'The Wiltshire Downs, then?' Tolkien suggested, 'or perhaps Scotland?'

'No', Lewis said, 'I prefer England; that's the tradition'.

'And the Quantock Hills?' Barfield opted, 'I've never been there, but I've heard it's beautiful.'

'Somerset is nice', Tolkien agreed, 'especially in spring'.

'In spring any region outside London or Oxford is nice!' Lewis exclaimed. They all laughed.

'I like the Quantocks', Williams continued. 'Maybe we can start our tour in Nether Stowey and visit the house of Coleridge. He used to live there for quite some time and wrote some of his best poetry there.'

'A splendid idea!' Barfield agreed. 'From there we can walk south, along the coast, to Exmoor.'

'Any objections?' Lewis asked.

They all lifted their glasses in agreement.

'Well then', Lewis concluded, 'The Quantocks it is!'

2

THE JOURNEY BEGINS

Nether Stowey, May 1938

The first half of May brought sunny days and scattered
rain. As expected, most of the showers came down in
the Northern Highlands and East Anglia, and almost
none in the West of Somerset. So in the third week of
May the outlook of a small journey in the Quantocks
was pretty good.

That morning the sun was up and the spirits were high.
The four Inklings had spent the night in Nether Stowey,
in *The Ancient Mariner*, an inn that dated back to the
sixteenth century. Located on Lime Street, almost
opposite the *Coleridge Cottage*, it was no surprise that
the Inn had taken the poet's most famous rhyme for its
name.

The previous day they had arrived in the village after a
long journey from Oxford. In the morning they had

taken the train South to Reading, where they changed trains in western direction to Taunton. From there they took the regional bus to Nether Stowey.

After breakfast they left their luggage at the inn and crossed Lime street to pay a visit to Coleridge Cottage. In the Victorian age it had been used as an inn, but from the start of the 20th century it was part of the National Trust and had been transformed into a museum. With its cream colored walls and mint green door and window frames it clearly distinguished itself from the other houses in the street. Inside they admired the way the original interior had been restored: the old table with the writing utensils, the fireplace with the armchair and the small library, the kitchen with the old dishes and outside even the vegetable garden flourished like in the old days.

'Unbelievable', Williams said, while looking around the garden. 'We're in the same place where Samuel Taylor Coleridge wrote his famous poems *Kubla Khan* and *The Rime of the Ancient Mariner*.'

Lewis turned to his companions and cited the poet: 'I fear thee, ancient Mariner! I fear thy skinny hand!' Barfield smiled and continued: 'And thou art long, and lank, and brown, as is the ribbed sea-sand.'

Lewis looked surprised and laughed. 'You know the poem well, Barfield!' And then added in a lower voice: 'For a lawyer....'

'Well', Barfield said, 'I do know my English poetry, of course. And I really love to read Coleridge. I even study him.'

'You study him', Tolkien repeated, 'and what for, if I may ask?

'Coleridge has some original ideas about the senses and the way we experience the world. It fascinates me.'
'Sounds interesting', Williams remarked, 'you should tell us some more about it.'
'Yes!' Lewis interrupted, 'very well, but not at this moment; we have to be on our way soon.'
And to Tolkien, somewhat further in the garden: 'Tollers, will you come with us?'
'Yes, yes', Tolkien said when he joined them in the house, 'I was just looking for the bower, but it seems to be gone.'
'Bower?' Lewis asked, 'what bower?'
Tolkien explained: 'The bower he writes about in the poem *This Lime-tree bower my prison*. Do you know the story? One day William Wordsworth and Charles Lamb come to visit him here. But what happened? His wife accidentally poured boiling milk over his foot, so he could only hobble in the garden to this bower. Imagine! Two famous poets came along and he couldn't go for a walk with them. What else could he do than write a poem about the bower, lamenting his fate?'
'That's a sad thing to hear', Lewis said, while walking with the others through the cottage, 'but at least it left us with another poem!'
They were all laughing when they left the historical building, discussing the relationship between human suffering and real art.
Outside they crossed the street and picked up their luggage at the inn.
In the first week of May when they were making preparations for the journey, Lewis had made sure that they would all use a 'rucksack', as he called it.

And so they left 'The Ancient Mariner' each with a rucksack on their back, on the way to the Quantock Hills. No provisions were taken for lunch or drinks, as Lewis insisted on halting at as many pubs along the road as possible.

They walked down Lime street to the red-brick clock tower with the sky-blue clock-face and then turned into Castle street. Soon they reached the outskirts of the village. From there the road moved uphill, to the remains of Stowey Castle. On top of the hill they only found a few of the foundations of the proud castle, by now fully overgrown by grasses and other plants. It was an eerie place, full of memories and ghosts of a time long gone by. The wind was stronger here and seemed to whisper stories of forgotten noblemen and slain knights.
Our four travelers, however, paid no attention to the historic mount they were standing on. Instead, they were clearly impressed by the view of the landscape: the endless tapestry of heath- and woodlands, scattered villages, hamlets and forests, and in the far distance the silver blue of the Bristol Channel.
'What a magnificent view!' Barfield uttered, regaining his breath after the climb to the top.
'Indeed', Tolkien added, and pointing his finger to the north: 'you can even see the Bristol Channel!' They all looked north and admired the view of the sea and the drifting clouds.
Then Williams turned and said: 'Look, you can see as far as Glastonbury Tor.' And showing them the direction: 'It's right there, at the horizon.'

In the east they saw the vague contours of a monumental tower on a small hill top.

'By Jove, you're right!' Lewis confirmed, his hand shielding his eyes from the sun. 'You can clearly see it.'

'The Isle of Avalon', Tolkien said in a solemn tone, 'or Ynys Wydryn as it is called in Celtic.'

'Isn't that the place where King Arthur is said to be buried?' Barfield asked.

'That's what they say', Tolkien answered. 'There are old texts which mention the discovery of the coffins of Arthur and Guinevere beneath the Glastonbury Tor at the end of the 12th century.'

'Texts....but neither hard facts nor artefacts to be shown in a museum', Lewis said.

'I'm afraid not', Tolkien continued, 'but there are also other legends and myths connected to this Tor. It is also said to be the place where the Holy Grail is hidden. And what's more: it's supposed to be the entrance to Annwn, the Land of the Fairies. Some kind of gateway to the realms of Gwyn ap Nudd, the legendary Lord of the Otherworld and King of the Fairies. He appears as a warlord with a blackened face in many of the narratives of the Black Book of Carmarthen'.

'Well', Williams began, 'it all sounds very interesting to me, especially for a Taliesin-admirer.' And looking up to his companions: 'So why don't we go that way?'

'Oh no', Lewis interrupted, shaking his head, 'that's not what we're going to do. We stick to our plan and I suggest we move forward now, or else we never get to Bicknoller today.'

'You're quite right', Barfield said and gesturing with an open arm: 'shall we, gentlemen? Somewhere over there a pub is waiting for us....'

They laughed and as they walked downhill Tolkien said to Williams: 'With a bit of luck, you may encounter your Gwyn ap Nudd after all. There's a legend in this region about a hooded horseman without a face, accompanied by several black dogs. Maybe we meet him along the way.'

Williams smiled. 'I'm not sure if I'd like to meet this creature; certainly not his dogs. And when he really has no face, how then does one communicate with this horseman?'

'I really don't know', Tolkien answered, 'that remains to be seen.'

They walked in silence further downhill and then followed a path above the stream that flowed from Castle Mount.

After several gates and a beautiful hedged lane, the road went uphill again. It took some effort to keep their original pace and soon it became apparent that Williams was a lot older and less trained than the others.

'Are you all right, Williams?' Barfield asked, 'or shall we lower the pace?'

Williams stopped for a moment, took a deep breath and managed to say: 'No, I'm all right, let's see that we get to Holford before lunch.'

Lewis couldn't agree more: 'I can barely wait for our 'Mittag-Essen' pub. Or at least a nice place to soak.'

They reached the edge of a forest and soon they entered Shervage Wood, a world almost completely made up of oak trees. In the forest there was hardly any wind and from that moment on they walked in the shadows, with only a little diffused light from the sun.

'Oak trees!' Tolkien exclaimed, raising his hands. 'Are they not a wonderful species?' He halted and put his hands on the trunk of one of the bigger trees. 'Rooted firmly in the earth and with their top reaching for the heavens. No wonder Oak trees were divine for Celtic and German tribes.'
'As far as I know, that's what all trees do', Lewis remarked.
Tolkien pretended he hadn't heard this and when he joined his companions he told them: 'In my view trees are some kind of co-creators of our world. What's more, I'm considering to give them a special role in 'The new hobbit'.'
'You mean, as a living creature?' Williams asked.
'Yes, something like that; I'm not sure yet.' And elaborating further: 'I think trees have a life of their own, like we have, only their sense of time is quite different.'
'That's certainly true', Barfield affirmed, 'after all, they grow more slowly and become older than we do. It's always strange to imagine that some of these trees have witnessed to the War of the Roses.'
They walked along the path that now led them through a darker part of the forest. Here the vegetation was more dense and the trees sometimes seemed to embrace the travelers.
'I never really like these places', Williams confessed, bowing his head to avoid a branch, 'it feels like the trees are closing in on us and watching everything we do.'

'Well, who knows?' Lewis said, teasing his companion, 'maybe it's an enchanted forest.'

'Aye', Tolkien added, 'with elves and dwarfs and all kind of underworld creatures.'

Williams looked hurt for a moment and then smiled. 'Look, it's just that I'm more fond of landscapes with a distant horizon, where you can see a tower or a hill to get your bearings. In a forest like this I feel more likely to get lost.'

'It's okay, Williams', Lewis said, patting his companion on the shoulder, 'It's okay.' And then smiling: 'Just stay with us.'

And with these words he took the lead again, yelling 'Let's go, gentlemen!'

Lewis had a map he consulted every ten minutes and he consequently ignored every trail to the left. As the intensity of daylight grew, the path emerged from the woods onto broad heathland.

The sun was warm now, in spite of some small clouds moving high in the sky.

Every now and then they took a few sips from their water flasks. And although the liquid lessened their thirst, it also awoke a desire for something stronger.

'How far till the next pub?' Barfield asked.

Lewis gestured with his hand and said: 'About two miles, I hope'.

Next he started to reproach Tolkien's ongoing interest in anything alive on this planet.

'You're a damned Coalbiter, Tollers', Lewis began, 'your everlasting love for little plants and crawling creatures takes up too much of our time.'

'Ah, the usual quack!' Tolkien sneered, for he had heard this comment many times before, during other walking tours. 'And of course you didn't notice that the wood was full of holly and lovely whortleberries? Of course, you couldn't see the berries yet and we are too late now for the flowers, but the bushes were definitely there.'
He walked on, mumbling to himself and then again turned to Lewis: 'Just be glad that the Gurt Wurm didn't find you'.
'The what?' Lewis asked, not understanding what he just heard.
'The Gurt Wurm, or Gurt Wyrm in old English, meaning 'great dragon'. The story goes that he lived in Shervage Wood and no doubt roamed the surrounding fields.'
And then as a kind of warning: 'we're quite visible and vulnerable walking through this heathland, you know.'
'I see', Barfield said, not at all intimidated, 'you're talking about the local Smaug?'
Williams chuckled and then asked: 'You mean Smaug was based on the story of the Gurt Wurm?'
'Oh no, not at all', Tolkien answered, 'I was inspired by old Norse Mythology; the Icelandic Volsunga Saga about the dwarf Fafnir who became a dragon and later was slain by the hero Sigurd.'
Lewis shook his head. 'Poor dragons', he said, 'in the end they all get killed. It seems they only live on in made up stories.'
'Oh, but now you're making a big mistake, Jack', Tolkien said. 'These stories are not just 'made up' for fun or entertainment. Like all myths, sagas and legends, they are told and retold to make sense of the world. I think there is an inherent truth in them.'

17

Lewis stopped for a moment and then turned to his companion. 'You really mean to say there were once dragons on this earth?'

'Who knows?' Tolkien answered, ' I have no proof of any paleontological findings or some Lost World where they still live, but I have noticed the dragon theme in many stories from all over the world. The same goes for the image in heraldry.'

'That's true', Barfield said, 'it surely must have some origin somewhere.'

Talking about the reality of dragons and the truth in myths, they climbed Woodlands Hill slowly, but gradually. And reaching the top with the large cairn, they had another magnificent view of the Bristol Channel and the surrounding heathlands.

'Look', Williams said, pointing to the north-west, 'that must be Holford. Can't be very far now'.

'Right', Lewis added, starting to descend towards the village, 'let's find ourselves a pint'.

Downhill they passed an old silk mill before reaching the first cottages of the village. A few minutes later they found 'the right place to soak' - in the words of Lewis: an old pub, called 'The Plough Inn'. They seated themselves at the tables outside and ordered the local Exmoor Ale. In addition Lewis asked for some bread, butter and cheese. 'Second breakfast' he grinned at his companions. Williams lit a cigarette, while the others stuffed their pipes. When their pints arrived, they were all puffing. 'Ah,' Barfield exclaimed after his first sip, 'beer can really be a blessing these days.'

'So it is', Tolkien agreed.

Lewis enjoyed his beer as well and then said: 'did you know Leonard and Virginia Woolf stayed in this inn for two days in 1912, during their honeymoon?'

'No, I didn't know', Williams answered, 'but I was in the Quantocks as well, during my honeymoon. Well, not in Holford, but in a village called Aisholt, a bit more to the south. Michal and I had met a lady called Olive Willis in 1917 - she's the founder of Down House, the exclusive girls' school - and she was kind enough to let us stay in her lovely cottage. I remember there was this fragrant rosemary bush in front of the house.' He smiled at the memory and continued: 'We made many walks and we passed through Holford too, as far as I can recall.'

They all ate eagerly from the buttered bread and cheese and ordered another beer. Barfield went inside to 'powder his nose'.

When he came back he looked a bit worried. 'I'm afraid I have some bad news, gentlemen', he said to his companions when he reached their table. 'The inn-keeper just told me that there have been strong indications that the German army is concentrating troops near the border with Czechoslovakia. Today the Czechs have mobilized more reservists and sent additional troops to the border.'

'That's bad news indeed', Lewis agreed. 'Any reactions from London or Paris?'

'Not yet, as far as I know', Barfield answered, 'but I suppose they are bound to react very soon, wouldn't you say?'

'They must', Tolkien said firmly. 'If we don't stand up to this aggression now, I'm sure we will come to regret it later.'

'But', Williams objected, 'aren't you afraid we are being dragged into a war with Germany? As far as I've heard we are not very well prepared yet for military conflict.'

'If the Germans think we are bluffing, they are bound to occupy the Sudetenland in any case', Lewis said.

Barfield nodded his head in agreement: 'Wasn't it a Prussian general who said war is but the continuation of politics, only with different means?'

'That may all be well and true', Tolkien said, 'but this madman has to be stopped.' He raised his voice when he continued: 'Gentlemen! If we let them conquer all of Europe, where would that leave us in the end? Fighting on our own, with our backs to the Atlantic? Never! If we want to stop this evil we have to do it now, before it grows too strong!'

'I agree with Tollers', Lewis admitted. 'I mean, I really dispise war; you all know that. But if it is inevitable, then we really should have the courage to go to war, even if we aren't quite prepared.'

'Hear, hear', Barfield said and banged with his fist on the table.

After that they fell silent for a few moments and smoked their pipes, each lost in their own thoughts.

The sun had already left its highest point when they continued their walk. Next stop would be the village of West-Quantoxhead, better known as St. Audries. Williams instantly regretted his second pint, feeling a bit light-headed when he moved. He was glad his companions hadn't noticed and decided to be more modest next time.

The sun was still warm, but a slight breeze made the weather quite pleasant. They left the village and walked along a path by the edge of the woods. After some time they passed the gates of a large estate, with a beautiful house in the middle of the courtyard.

'Ah', Lewis said, 'this must be Alfaxdon Manor; the house where William and Dorothy Wordsworth stayed for a year in 1797 and 1798. This is where he wrote most of his Lyrical Ballads.'

They admired the classic architecture of the house, surrounded by a park full of trees.

'Yes, I remember we passed this house during one of our walks in 1918', Williams said. And turning to his companions: 'Did you know they only paid 23 pounds rent for a whole year? Imagine! This whole manor for just the two of them.'

Barfield smiled and added: 'It looks like big buildings give room to big ideas. On the other hand, poor old Coleridge was scribbling his greatest poems in his tiny cottage.'

Tolkien stepped forward, pointing his finger at Barfield. 'Talking about Coleridge; earlier today you said you study him for some reason. Maybe now is the time to tell us a bit more about that.'

Barfield nodded and said: 'I would be glad to explain my fascination with Coleridge to you.'

As they walked on through a vast area of heathland, Barfield tried to explain some of Coleridge's ideas to his companions: 'Coleridge was a poet as well as a philosopher. He constructed his own view on reality and of the way we experience the world. And whatever it was, it certainly wasn't the Cartesian view. As you know, Descartes made a fundamental difference between the object that we observe and the subject that we are. It is this separation of the observer from the observed, that Coleridge rejects. Because that worldview has been taught as the only truth. We grew up with it. Just as medieval people grew up with the elements and the idea that hierarchy, luck and love were all God-given gifts. Just as prehistoric man had an even more different view of the world. The more I study these ideas, the more I realize, that the way we LEARN to look, to listen and to smell, determines the way we experience the world.'

The path had lead them downhill, to a point where they could cross the stream. From the bridge they could see the water shining in the sun, on its way to the sea. On the other side of the stream was more heathland to cross, then another stream, and then a path upwards to the woodlands that surrounded the village of West Quantoxhead.

'For Coleridge', Barfield continued, 'there is no separation between observer and observed. OUR experience of the world IS reality. The direct perception of the world leads to what Coleridge calls the primary imagination. That world of the senses is the world we share with all other people and it leads to a basic level of understanding, with functions like memory and logic. But according to Coleridge there is also a higher level of understanding. Through imagination, intuition and poetic inspiration, it is connected to the highest level of awareness and that is Reason. Reason is almost God-like. It is the beginning and the end of all that is. And we can only comprehend a fraction of it.'

'I see', Williams said, 'and when souls meet on the level of imagination, where they share a fraction of the divine, would you call that a matter of co-inherence?'

Barfield nodded his head: 'Yes, indeed I would. If Coleridge had known your concept in his days, he surely would have used it.'

Williams seemed satisfied. Then Tolkien said: 'In the realm of imagination, we mortals are nothing but sub-creators under the divine will.'

Barfield agreed: 'You certainly can say that, although Coleridge went even further. We think we create our stories and poems ourselves. Coleridge claims that in the realm of imagination we are guided by another, higher source of inspiration. In that way we are really sub-creators.'

They crossed the second stream and slowly started climbing uphill to the woods in the distance.

'Don't worry, Williams', Lewis said, 'the path leads through a very small part of the forest.'

Williams didn't answer. He probably hadn't even heard Lewis, as he was concentrating on his steps, climbing the hill to the next village. He was sweating and promised himself he would only drink tea there and avoid beer.

'Everything all right, Williams?' Barfield asked, noticing his companion sometimes made unsteady steps.

Williams nodded in silence, sparing his breath for the walk.

'I was wondering', Lewis started, referring to the earlier discussion, 'if all imagination is guided by some sort of divine inspiration, then how is it possible that we all use the element of evil in our stories? Surely that can't come from divine inspiration or be the purpose of sub-creation?'

'I think I know the answer to that', Tolkien said, taking a pause from the walk. 'I suppose evil is an integral part of the realm of Man. Like it or not, it is all part of the grand design and It is our mission to come to terms with the evil in our world and in ourselves. That's why it plays a role in our stories. Besides', and he started to laugh, 'Without evil our stories would be rather dull, wouldn't they?'

The others laughed and agreed with Tolkien's explanation.

They reached the edge of St. Audries Forest and the shadows of the trees were a blessing after the climb in the afternoon sun. This time they were surrounded by pine trees, although the path stayed close to the edge of the forest. With a large bend it turned left and then went downhill again. Before they knew it they were out of the forest and nearing the first cottages of the village. Williams stopped, took a thick book from his rucksack and read out loud: 'It is called West Quantoxhead if we go by the map, but it is St. Audries to everybody.' His companions smiled and looked inquisitively. ' So, what book is that, Williams?' Tolkien asked.

Williams showed the dark blue cover with the white image and letters. It was the Somerset edition of The King's England series by Arthur Mee.

'Ah!' Tolkien said, 'I knew it would be something like that. Mee is well-known for these series.'

'You mean you carried this voluptuous reference book all the way in your rucksack?' Lewis asked.

'Well yes, I did', Williams answered, 'you never know how it can be of use, don't you?'

Lewis took the book and shook his head while browsing through the 500 pages with descriptions of every town and village in Somerset. 'I'm glad we only visit a handful of these places', he said and returned the book to Williams.

Within five minutes they were sitting on the terrace of the Windmill pub, with a beautiful view of the old church in a green park, surrounded by hills full of trees. Behind these trees, they knew, were the coast and the Bristol Channel.

Lewis ordered a pint for everyone and Williams was just in time to change his order into 'a nice cup of tea'.

They all enjoyed the rest after hours of climbing and descending in the Quantock Hills. Williams was sipping his tea and glancing through his big blue book.

'Anything on Bicknoller?', Barfield asked.

'No, not really', Williams answered, 'mostly a description of the interior of the 15th century church.'

'I say', Tolkien started, pointing to the hills, 'if the coast is right on the other side of these hills, why don't we walk up there and have a nice view of the Bristol Channel?'

'That would certainly be nice, Tollers', Lewis said, 'but I'm afraid it would take too much time.

This morning we began with a visit to Coleridge cottage and therefore we are a little behind on our schedule. It's not a big problem, but I would like to get to Bicknoller before sunset.'

Tolkien nodded; 'You're quite right, Jack', he said, 'besides, we've already had a lovely view of the Channel twice.'

Having finished their pints and tea, they all picked up their rucksacks and set out on the last part of the journey for that day.

'Can't be more than two miles now', Lewis said.

'Great!' Tolkien grunted, 'I'm getting hungry!'

'You sound like a real hobbit', Barfield said, smiling.

'Well, it's true', Tolkien admitted, 'I am every inch a hobbit, except in size. I like all things they like - gardens, trees, my pipe-tobacco and of course food and beer.' He paused and then added: 'And I hate adventures...'

They laughed after hearing this honest statement. In fact, it probably applied to the others as well.

They walked along the edge of some more woodlands and were happy to see the path descending.

Lewis again took the lead, map in his hand, to make sure they would keep up the pace.

After some time, Williams asked Barfield: 'Talking about Coleridge's worldview, when he states that our experience IS reality, would you say he ignores things we can't (yet) see or hear? I mean, the purely scientific approach means that all you can't measure, doesn't exist. Isn't Coleridge's approach doing the same?'

'That's an interesting question', Barfield said, 'but I think there's a big difference between modern science and Coleridge when it comes to things 'unknown' or 'invisible'. In the eyes of science they just don't exist, that's true. But for Coleridge, when these phenomena are part of our experience, through intuition, imagination or sixth sense, they are a reality. Do hobbits exist?
Not according to science. But when we read about Bilbo Baggins and his adventures, they are very alive to us and part of our experience.'

'I like the idea', Tolkien said, 'it's quite a different way of experiencing reality.'

Lewis consulted his map and decided they had to turn right. The others gladly followed, knowing Lewis had a special talent for finding pubs and 'places to soak' in every surrounding.

They were not disappointed, for after a few minutes they entered Bicknoller where they would enjoy a good meal and stay the night.

3

THUNDER IN THE FOREST

Bicknoller, May 1938

After a good night's sleep they had breakfast together in the dining room. Passing the butter to Barfield, Lewis started: 'I have some good and I have some bad news this morning, gentlemen. What will it be first?'

'Then give us the bad news first', Tolkien suggested, 'so we can continue with the good.'

'Right', Lewis agreed, 'the bad news - well, not very bad in fact - is that the weather will not be as nice as yesterday. You've probably noticed that there are clouds coming in from the sea and there's a good chance there will be some rain today; maybe even a thunderstorm.' He looked around at his companions, waiting for a reaction.

Barfield was the first: 'I guess we'll survive, won't we? So what is the good news?'

'Yes, Jack', Williams added, 'Tell us the good news!'
'Well', Lewis muttered, eating some bread, 'the good news is, that today we will not have to climb as much as we did yesterday. The path is relatively flat, except for the part right after we pass Monksilver. At that point we have to climb 'Bird's Hill', but after that the path mostly descends.'

Williams smiled, 'That sounds like a blessing to me', he said.

The others agreed; yesterday's walk had given them all a bit of muscle ache.

'Speaking of news', Barfield began, 'I just heard that London and Paris have sent warnings to Berlin. In the event of a German attack on Czechoslovakia both France and Britain will intervene.'

'Oh my God', Tolkien said, 'they really did that?'

Williams shook his head and said: 'I just can't believe this is all happening again. I mean, not another war.'

'It's not war yet', Barfield said, 'but you're right; those aren't peaceful statements either.'

'Well, they shouldn't be peaceful at all', Tolkien grumbled, 'I'm afraid it's the only language Mr. Hitler understands...'

'You're probably right', Williams agreed, 'but what happens if he calls our bluff?'

Tolkien sighed and said: 'I just hope we never find out'.

Lewis shook his head. 'It all seems like a strange kind of nightmare. How can a civilized country like Germany - or Prussia - fall back into such a state of barbarism? I mean, for many years we looked eastward for great composers, artists and philosophers. The Teutons brought us Beethoven, Brahms and Wagner.'

'Don't forget Goethe and Schiller', Barfield added.
'I guess the Italians are just as bad', Williams claimed,
'and yet they brought us Roman Law and the works of
Dante.'
'It's all very complicated and confusing', Lewis
recapitulated, 'and we surely live in dangerous times.
Therefore, gentlemen, I suggest we focus on our own
road ahead.'
He stood up and addressed his travel companions: 'Let's
go! Take your rucksacks and follow me. We have to get
to Roadwater today'.

Outside they noticed dark clouds coming in from the sea.
Above them the clouds took all kinds of forms, from
dragons and orcs to castles and mountains.
'The weather is quite different, today', Williams
remarked, 'no sunshine; just clouds and wind.'
'Well, I suppose we're prepared for that', Lewis said,
tapping his old hat. He studied his map and then pointed
his finger. 'It's this way', he said, taking the lead.
They left the village and took a path through the fields,
extending as far as the eye could see.

After some time they crossed a single railway track.
'This must be the West Somerset Railway', Lewis said.
'It starts in Taunton and goes all the way to the coast.
Mostly used in the holiday season, I expect.'
Next to the railway track was a stream that ran almost
parallel to the iron road. They crossed the stream and
continued on a path through the fields.
'You know', Lewis started, 'I have been here before. I
mean, in this region, like Williams after his wedding. It

was in the summer of 1921, but only for a few days. And I wasn't on foot; instead we drove a four-seater Wolseley motor car. The car belonged to uncle Gussie and aunt Anne and we drove all the way from the Cotswolds to the Quantocks. We passed here through Williton, a bit more to the west and then on to Minehead and Porlock. It was a nice ride, but the problem was that every now and then we had car trouble. So we had to stay in Dunster and later in Porlock, because the mechanics had to fix the car.'

'A Wolseley', Barfield said, 'that's an oldie! Must have been fun, driving a car like that in summer.'

'It was', Lewis admitted, 'but I prefer to walk these hills.

They walked on along the stream, and passed some woodlands and the hamlet of Woolston.

Suddenly Williams stopped, pointing his finger to the ground.

'Look! A frog!'

Tolkien looked and then shook his head.

'No Williams, that's definitely not a frog. It's a toad.'

'A toad?' Williams said. He looked surprised and then smiled: 'maybe it's not even a toad.'

'What do you mean?' Tolkien asked.

'Come on, Tolkien, think magical, like in fairy tales. This toad just might be a prince!'

They all laughed and Tolkien said: 'Well, prince or not, I'm not going to kiss it.'

'Ah, then he is doomed', Lewis concluded, 'to stay a toad for the rest of his life'.

'Maybe he's happy that way', Barfield suggested. And then, more seriously: 'Most important here, is the ability to see a prince in a frog. That is how you create a magical world: by looking at things differently, just as Coleridge did.'

'You're quite right', Lewis said, 'but critics will call it escapism'.

'Ah, the critics!' Tolkien snorted, 'I always become furious when I hear such statements. Because it's just the opposite. When we imagine another world - like the world of faerie - it's because we want to look further than the narrow world view of critics and scientists. That's not escapism.'

'Indeed it isn't', Williams added, 'in the realm of imagination and through co-inherence we discover the deep structures of creation and the meaning of life.'

'Well said', Barfield applauded.

Meanwhile, the wind became stronger and the clouds grew thicker and darker. They all donned their hats now and it didn't take long before the first raindrops fell on their rucksacks.

'Typical English weather', Barfield complained, holding his hat with his hand, 'first day it makes you sweat, next day it makes you wet'.

'Don't complain, Barfield', Lewis interrupted, 'it's not raining yet - in fact, it's not raining at all. These are just some spots to remind us of the elements.'

'Nice talking', Tolkien said, 'may then the elements be with us, for I hate to see my clothes get drenched.'

They walked on, blessed by a few raindrops and after some time entered the village of Sampford Brett. The

32

first thing they noticed was the beautiful old church with the square tower.

Lewis saw Williams studying his book and asked: 'Anything on the church, Williams?'

Williams nodded. 'Yes, actually. The church is 13th century and inside is a stone figure of a knight. It's from the grave of the Lord of Sampford Brett, Richard de Brett. He was one of the bloodstained knights who murdered Thomas Becket on the steps of the altar of Canterbury cathedral.'

'Well, well, well', Lewis said, and then, shaking his head, 'killing a bishop isn't what you'd call a noble act, would you? Then I see no reason why we should honor him with a visit. What do you think, gentlemen?'

'I think you're right', Tolkien replied, 'we'd better find ourselves a pub instead.'

Barfield had walked on and now returned with the grave news.

'I'm afraid it might be very difficult - if not impossible - to find a pub here.

I looked around the corner and there was no sign of a pub and not much of a village either.'

'Hey, boy!' Tolkien shouted to a boy who was just running by at the other side of the road. 'Is there a pub here?'

'No sir', the boy replied, 'not around here'. And then pointing to the road behind them: 'But there is one in Bicknoller!'

The boy ran on and disappeared in one of the houses.

'Bicknoller!' Tolkien grunted, 'that's where we came from!'

Lewis was outraged. 'Can you believe it?' he cried out,
'a village without a pub? How do these people live?'
And then, gesturing with his arm: 'This whole village is
cursed - it must be - thanks to Richard the bishop
slayer!'
In spite of the bad news they laughed and checked their
rucksacks to continue the journey.
'Well then', Lewis said, 'we'd better step up the pace to
get to the pub in Monksilver then.'

They left the village, walking along the road that led
them into the fields. Fortunately the sun now peeked
through the clouds so they could all enjoy the beautiful
scenery of the valley they were walking through. It was a
true English landscape that would have inspired any
British composer to write an unforgettable pastoral
symphony.
Lewis walked in front, as usual, now and then studying
his map. Barfield went to walk next to him and asked:
'By the way, Lewis, do you believe in curses?'
Lewis smiled and gave it some thought. Then he said:
'That's an interesting question, Barfield. We write about
spells and curses in our stories, so why shouldn't we
believe in their existence?'
Barfield smiled in return: 'You're not answering my
question.'
Lewis sighed and said 'You'd better ask Williams then,
he's with the Crowley circus and knows everything
about spells, curses and black magic.'
Williams happened to overhear their discussion and
interrupted irritated:

'That's not fair, Lewis; you say this time and time again and it just isn't true. I had nothing to do with Crowley and when the Order split I joined Waite in the Rectified Rite of the Golden Dawn. And later I followed Waite to the Fellowship of the Rosy Cross, because you know just as well as I do, that the Order ceased to exist in 1915.'

'All right, all right', Lewis said, raising his hands in defense, 'but you do know a lot about spells and curses, don't you? I mean, the leaders of the Order always claimed they had secret knowledge of occult powers.'

'Well, I don't really know about that. There was a lot of talk in certain circles in London and Crowley loved it. I prefer the vision of Waite: the Order was too obsessed with the concept of power; in the Fellowship we focus on mystic knowledge to deepen our understanding of Creation.'

Barfield nodded, in acknowledgement. Then he returned to his original subject: 'Let me rephrase my question: are there also good spells and curses? I mean, are they always evil, or is there also something good like the spell of the fairy in Cinderella?'

'If I may interject, gentlemen', Tolkien said, joining his fellow travelers, 'I'd say there is no such thing as white or black magic. It's a tool and it all depends on the intention of the person who uses it. You can't say a gun is good or evil - it depends on what you do with it. In The New Hobbit, for instance, the wizard Gandalf supports the good forces in the world, but even a wizard can be corrupted by power. It all depends on how he acts.'

They walked on through the valley, glad that the sun had returned and that the path was not as steep as yesterday. In the fields they saw all kinds of flowers and in the distance groups of trees. Around them was the chatter of birds and the buzzing of insects and in the sky the lonely flight of a bird of prey.

After they crossed another road, Williams asked: 'Talking about The New Hobbit, will there also be fairies, besides hobbits, orcs and elves?'

'Oh, no!' Tolkien answered a little bit shocked, 'of course there won't be fairies!'

He lowered his voice and explained: 'I use the word 'Faery' only to indicate a mythical world that we can enter through stories or intuition. The creatures you have in mind are more fancy than faery and are cherished by the same 'circles' in London you mentioned earlier. Do you remember the romantic fairy pictures of Conan Doyle? Well, believe me, they don't have anything to do with the world of faery.'

'When we write a story', Lewis took over, 'we create a secondary world that is convincing as long as the spell is not broken. And the spell is stronger when that world is rooted in myth.'

'Indeed', Tolkien added, 'we even made it our mission to create new myths, because that was exactly what our literature lacks. North European mythology can be traced back to Norse and Icelandic saga's; but the earliest texts we have are the Arthurian legends.'

At that moment Lewis made a sharp turn to the right and announced that they were almost in Monksilver. 'It's over there, right behind those trees', he said, pointing his finger to the end of the slowly descending road.

'At last!' Williams sighed, 'I'm dying for a smoke.'

'And I'm in for a beer', Barfield said, a suggestion that was agreed upon by the others. They entered the village close to the church and nearby found the Notley Arms pub where they could rest their feet and quench their thirst.

After a beer, a smoke and some bread they all felt much better. Only Williams stuck with his usual cup of tea, knowing that after Monksilver there would be one more hill to climb.

'You know', Williams said, 'there's a funny story connected to Monksilver. It's about Francis Drake and his love for a certain lady Elizabeth. She promised to marry him, but after he sailed away there was no word from him for months. She fell in love with another man, but on her wedding day a big cannon ball fell from the sky. It was probably some kind of meteorite, but for her it was a sign that Drake was on his way back home. The marriage was postponed and in the end she married Drake.'

'That's a remarkable story', Barfield said, 'and a good example of the way the heavens can intervene in our earthly matters.'

When they left the pub, the clouds casted long shadows over the valley. The wind was strong again and they all raised the collars of their jackets.

'How far is it to Roadwater?' Tolkien asked.

'About four and a half miles', Lewis answered, 'but with a steep climb through the forest to Bird's Hill'.

With that in mind they put on their hats and rucksacks and followed Lewis in the direction of the forest.

Soon the path started to lead uphill and as the effort took most of their breath there wasn't much talking. They entered the forest that consisted mostly of oak trees. With the clouds above them and no sunshine to be seen, the forest looked darker and more sinister than the woods of the day before. Williams felt uneasy, of course, but did his best not to show this. Lewis concentrated on the path ahead, climbing the hill with a disciplined semi-professional pace.

When they passed a sign 'Bird's Hill', Lewis waved them on with his hand, saying that they hadn't reached the highest point yet.

At last the line of trees ended and from there a beautiful landscape unfolded before their eyes. When the weather conditions were good you could see as far as the Bristol Channel. But on that moment all they could see were more and darker clouds coming in from the sea.

'I suggest we move on', Lewis said, 'and as the path mostly descends from here, we can make some progress. I expect some rain the next hours.'

In silence they agreed with Lewis' proposal and started the descend to Sticklepath and Pit Wood.

At first the descent was a welcome change of motion, after more than an hour of climbing. They walked swiftly downhill on the small pathway and were happy with the advance they made. Some even got hope they would reach Roadwater before the rain would start to fall.

But then they began to feel their legs and most of all their knees.

'Can we walk a bit more slowly downhill', Williams suggested, 'I have this increasing pain in my knees.' Lewis, who already was ten steps ahead of the others, said: 'If we slow down our pace now, we may end up in a thunderstorm.' And with these words he continued the descend at the same pace.

'Jack!' Barfield shouted.

Lewis stopped, turned and looked up.

'I agree with Williams', Barfield said, 'If we don't take our steps a bit more carefully, we will all end up with muscle ache. And we'll be only halfway once we reach Roadwater, so we still have a long way to go. Besides, the path is also muddy here and there. I wouldn't like to see one of us fall.'

'All right, all right', Lewis said, waving is hand, 'I'll lower the pace.'

They marched further in silence, each with his own thoughts on walking, the weather and the world. Finally they reached the end of the forest and found themselves in the hamlet of Sticklepath. Dark clouds gathered over the village and the valley and the first drops of rain began to fall when they passed through the only street of the little township.

'I don't expect to find a pub in this godforsaken village', Tolkien said, 'but maybe we can find a place where we can find shelter from the rain.'

'You call this rain?' Lewis reacted, mocking his friend's suggestion. 'This is not even drizzle, Tollers, so I intend to keep on walking till we are in Roadwater.'

Tolkien didn't answer. He pulled his hat firmly over his head and followed in Lewis' footsteps. The others did the same.

After the last descent they walked straight through the open fields. The wind drove the rain in their faces, their eyes and their clothes. The path was muddy now and slippery, so they had to watch their footing.

'It's like the Somme again', Tolkien muttered, 'I hate mud, I hate rain and most of all the combination of the two'.

Barfield grunted a confirmation. 'They say it's a blessing for the farmers and the flowers. Well, I agree, but I don't like my clothes getting soaking wet. We may just as well take a swim...'

Tolkien laughed and so did Williams, who had just wiped the rain from his glasses.

Lewis didn't hear them talking, as he was far ahead of them.

Suddenly a flash of lightning illuminated the valley and in the distance they could see the first trees of Pit Wood. Then came the loud rumble of the thunder.

Williams shook his head and said: 'I won't enter the forest when there's a thunderstorm. It's just too dangerous.'

'I agree', Barfield said, 'but how do we tell Lewis?'

He put a hand next to his mouth and yelled: 'Jack! Wait!'

Through the falling rain they could see the figure of Lewis stop and turn around. He raised his arms as if he was saying 'What now?'

When they reached Lewis, the rain was dripping from their hats and Lewis asked: 'What is it?'

'Well', Barfield said, looking at his companions, 'we'd like to find some shelter against the rain.' And then, directly to Lewis: 'Look, we don't mind getting a bit wet, walking along the path. But soaking wet is another story.'

'Quite', Tolkien agreed, 'if we just keep on walking like dumb animals, surely one of us will catch a cold.

'Nonsense!', Lewis cried out, gesturing with his hand as if killing some insects. 'You call yourselves real men? If we're all that faint at heart we'll never win another war!'

'Jack', Williams said, ' you saw the lightning; it's not wise to enter the forest now.'

Lewis shook his head and then raised his arms to catch the rain. 'Look!' he said, 'this is Nature! These are the elements! It's all part of creation and we too are part of it, whether you like it or not.'

'That may all be true', Tolkien said, 'but we are going to look for shelter. There must be something like a farm around here.'

'Suit yourself!' Lewis sneered and turned in the direction of the forest. 'I'm on my way to Roadwater and you are a bunch of unwilling hobbledehoys.'

And with these words he continued on the muddy path towards the forest.

'Jack!' Barfield yelled, 'be sensible!'

'I am!' Lewis answered, without slowing his pace.

Within a few minutes his figure faded into the distance and became part of the rain, the forest and the landscape.

The three companions looked at the disappearing Lewis and then at each other.

'Argh!' Tolkien growled, his arms raised in despair, 'That........man'.

Williams shook his head, scattering the raindrops from his hat.

'Typically Jack', he said, 'stubborn till the end.'

'I suggest we start looking for our shelter', Barfield
interrupted, 'there must be a farm somewhere.'
With that perspective in mind they walked a bit faster
along the path towards the forest. But instead of entering
Pit Wood, they took a road to the left. They passed some
kind of factory on their right and then saw in the
distance the contours of a neat row of trees, which often
indicates the existence of a farm.
'There!' Barfield said, pointing in the direction of the
trees. 'I think there's our farm!'
They walked to the trees and saw a courtyard with some
buildings. As soon as they reached the first barn, a dog
started barking. A door in the second building opened
and someone beckoned them to come in.
'Please, gentlemen', the woman said, 'do come in; the
weather is too bad!'
They gratefully accepted the invitation and followed her
into the living room.
'Thank you, Madam', Tolkien said, 'and please excuse us
for our wet clothes and shoes.'
'Oh, never mind', the woman answered, 'I'm used to that.
Shall I make you a nice cup of tea?'
'That would be lovely', Williams said, 'we're very
grateful.'
She smiled and left the room to boil some water.
They all took a seat at the table and felt the pain in their
legs caused by the descent from 'Bird's hill'. Outside
there was another flash of light, followed by thunder.
'I'm so glad we found this farm', Williams sighed.
'So am I', Tolkien agreed. 'I'm just a bit worried about
poor Jack, walking on his own in this horrible weather.'

'Well', Barfield said, 'let's hope for the best. If he keeps on walking in the right direction, he will reach Roadwater soon enough.'

At that moment the farmer entered the room, followed by his wife. He welcomed his unexpected guests, while she handed everyone a cup of tea and some biscuits. The warm liquid felt like a blessing for their battered bodies.

'Shall I light a fire?', the farmer asked, 'so you gentlemen can dry your clothes?'

'That's very kind of you', Barfield said, 'but we won't stay very long. We have to get to Roadwater today. So as soon as the rain stops we'll be on our way.'

'I see', the farmer said, lighting his pipe, 'and you're on holiday?'

They told him about their walking trip from Nether Stowey to Porlock, that they will be halfway when they reach Roadwater and that one of their companions had decided to carry on through the rain.

The farmer slowly shook his head. 'Don't worry', he said, 'he'll make it all right, but it's not a wise thing to do. Besides, there are strange creatures on the road nowadays.'

'Creatures?' Tolkien repeated, 'what do you mean? Riders without a face? Dragons perhaps?' The last words he almost spoke hopefully.

'No, no', the farmer answered, 'nothing like that, thank God. That's legend. No, you hear things about strange people visiting the region, dressed in weird clothes and mumbling strange words.'

'Well', Barfield said, 'we haven't seen them yet, but we'll be careful.'

And then they talked about the weather (which would be better), the coming war (no news from the farmer), and many other important issues, as if it was another Tuesday morning at the 'Bird and Baby'.

They stayed at the farm for another hour until the rain had stopped. The darkest clouds had drifted inland and the remaining cloud cover made way for the sun announcing better weather conditions.

They went outside and thanked the farmer and his wife for their hospitality.

'Take care, gentlemen', the farmer said, 'I do hope you have a pleasant journey!'

The three companions said goodbye and then headed for the road to Pit Wood and Roadwater.

In the forest the path was muddy and raindrops still fell from the trees. They took it all for granted, remembering the thunderstorm earlier in the afternoon. Luckily there was a main path through the forest, as Jack had taken the only map in their possession. They just hoped there would be a sign at the next crossroads, indicating the right way to Roadwater.

Strange creatures. The words of the farmer echoed in their heads and they noticed that at every bend of the path they were looking out for them. Williams even mentioned this feeling of 'being followed', but the others thought he was imagining things and attributed it to Williams' general feeling of uneasiness when he was walking in a forest.

'Maybe it's Jack', Barfield suggested, trying to make them laugh, 'waiting somewhere to scare us.'
His companions didn't find it funny, so they didn't laugh.
For the rest of their journey through the forest they walked on in silence.
After the woodlands there were open fields, where they were welcomed by the sun. At last they could dry their clothes a bit, while walking in the direction of Roadwater. The path was muddy now and then, so the slippery parts of the way were a greater risk to them than some unknown strange creature lurking in the woods.
They all wondered if Jack had found his way to Roadwater, but they would know soon enough. Within an hour they entered the village and found their way to 'The Valiant Soldier' pub. And of course Jack was there. He had changed his clothes and was drinking a beer and seemed not at all surprised to see them.
'Ah, there you are!' he said, 'you finally found your way up here!'
Barfield threw his hat and rucksack on the table and mumbled: 'Yes, indeed, Jack, and we did it all without a map. How's that?'
'Well, you have my compliments. At least your clothes aren't as wet as mine.'
'It's all a matter of choice, Jack', Tolkien said, 'not principle. But now, most of all, we'd like to wet our throats. I'm starving for a beer.'
And with that, the discussion was over and they ordered beer to celebrate their reunion.

4

THE NECROMANCER

Roadwater, May 1938

The next morning the weather was good. There were still
some clouds, but the sun was shining as well. They had
breakfast at a table near the window and were all
enjoying the sunny view outside.

'I think it's going to be a lovely day', Williams said, 'the
kind of day we deserve after yesterday's wet experience.'

'The weather is good', Jack said, 'but I'm afraid we will
have plenty of reason to feel hot along the way.'

'What do you mean?' Tolkien asked, sipping his tea.

'Well, there will be some serious climbing today', Lewis
explained, 'first from here through Langridge Woods
and then, after a descent to Luxborough, another climb
to Lype Hill. But', he added, 'with these weather
conditions, the views will be magnificent.'

'Well', Barfield said, 'at least that's something to look forward to.' And then, with a wink, 'and don't forget the strange creatures....'

Tolkien and Williams laughed, but Lewis didn't understand.

'You see, Jack,' Tolkien said, jokingly, 'you missed a lot...'

And then they told him about the stories the farmer had told them.

But Jack wasn't worried at all. 'Nonsense', he said, 'there have been strange people on the road since the beginning of time, so that won't stop us from continuing our trip, will it?'

'No, of course not', Barfield said, 'it was just a story we heard.'

'Right', Lewis said, 'and if we want to have a story to tell at home, we'll have to be on our way. So, gentlemen, get your rucksacks!'

After they left the village of Roadwater, they took the road with a sign indicating the direction of Luxborough. After half a mile they changed to a path going uphill and all the way through Langridge Wood.

This part of the forest consisted mostly of pine trees and firs. Through the gap in the trees above the path there was even enough room for the sun to come through, so the light was enough to make even Williams feel good that morning.

'This feels like the metaphysical forest of Broceliande', he remarked, 'the one I write about in 'Taliessin through Logres'. It's a place where things are created, both good and evil.'

'And how do you know which is which?' Barfield asked. 'Well', Williams answered, 'you never really know, do you? Not until something or someone expresses itself, in words or deeds. It's like the idea of magic we talked about: you can't call it good or evil until you know the intention of the person using it.'

They fell silent for some time, mostly because their attention was needed for the climbing. The path meandered through the forest and with each step they felt the weight of their rucksacks.

Now and then they heard the shuffling of small creatures between the trees and Williams couldn't help thinking about the warnings of the farmer.

Barfield stopped to sip some water and the others did the same. 'You know', Tolkien said, 'if Coleridge took this same route, he must have had strong legs.'

'Not only that', Barfield added, 'he also must have had some breath for reciting new poetry. Or do you think he wrote it all down, every moment a new line came to his mind?'

'In that case', Lewis said, 'he wouldn't get very far, would he?'

'Through wood and dale', Barfield recited, 'the sacred river ran,
 Then reached the caverns measureless to man,
 And sank in tumult to a lifeless ocean;
 And 'mid this tumult Kubla heard from far
 Ancestral voices prophesying war...'

'That's 'Kubla Khan', right?' Wiliams said.

'Indeed', Barfield said, 'and then came the Person from Porlock.'

'Who?' Lewis asked.

Barfield smiled. 'The story goes, that the poem 'Kubla Khan' was never really completed, because Coleridge was disturbed by this 'person from Porlock'. He had this great vision of a poem of more than a hundred pages, but it never was to be. Till this day there is discussion among scholars whether there really was a 'person from Porlock' or that he invented him, because he got stuck.'

'Interesting', Lewis said, 'and what do you think?'

Barfield smiled and said: 'I think he had a poet's block.'

'And I think', Tolkien said, 'he just hadn't enough breath to continue, while he was climbing these hills.'

'I suggest', Williams said, only just regaining his breath, 'that upon reaching Porlock we look for the descendants of this 'person'.'

'To thank them or to curse them?' Lewis asked.

They all laughed.

'I don't know yet', Williams confessed, 'but I'll think about it on the way.'

They drank from their water flasks and then continued the climb through the forest. They were thankful for the shade of the trees, as with every hour the sun became warmer.

Now and then the path was still muddy from the rains of the day before. Carefully they made their steps, sometimes wiping the sweat from their faces with their handkerchiefs.

Suddenly Williams stopped and said: 'Listen!' They all stopped and listened.

After a minute Lewis asked: 'What is it, Williams? Not the creature, I hope?'

Williams looked unhappy. 'No, I just thought I heard something.'

'Well', Lewis concluded, 'I hear nothing now, so it will be all right.'

And with these words he continued the path to the top of the hill.

It took some further effort but at last they came to the end of Langridge Wood. The path still went uphill, but now they walked through the open fields. After a few yards they stopped to admire the view of the beautiful landscape that unfolded before their eyes: the ever changing fields in green and yellow and on the horizon the blue and silver of the Bristol Channel.

'It's beautiful here', Williams said, blessing the wind coming from the sea.

'It certainly is', Barfield confirmed, 'from here you can look back at the Quantocks.'

They followed his view and saw the first half of their journey.

From where they stood the Coleridge Cottage looked very far.

'So', Lewis said, clasping his hands, 'those were the Quantocks, let's get on to Exmoor!'

'Oh, come on, Lewis', Barfield complained, 'stop the *kafuffle* for one time and let us enjoy the scenery. We climbed all our way up to see this.'

'All right, all right', Lewis said, 'but I'm dying to have a beer in Luxborough.'

'So are we', Barfield admitted, 'so are we.'

They stayed on top of the hill for another ten minutes
and then joined Lewis in the descent to Luxborough.
The path was wider than in the forest, so they could walk
side by side. Tolkien caught up with Lewis, who as
always was leading the way.

'A penny for your thoughts, Tollers', Lewis said,
'you've been quite silent for some time.'

'Ah, yes', Tolkien admitted, 'I must have been.
Actually, I was thinking of 'my little one' - my wife -
and how things will be at home.'

Lewis looked a bit worried. 'You're not getting
homesick, I hope?'

'Oh, no', Tolkien reassured his friend, 'not at all. We're
used to this, with all my work and my writing.'

'By the way', Lewis went on, 'did you know there was a
time when Oxford dons were not supposed to marry?'

Tolkien nodded his head, 'Yes, I heard about that. Funny
isn't it? In those days they were monks and hermits. And
nowadays we're a kind of hobbits, enjoying our meals,
our beer and our smoke.'

'You're right', Lewis continued, 'and we only lock
ourselves in our study to write about elves and dragons
and travels in outer-space. There are no adventures in
our daily lives.'

'Oh no!' Tolkien looked shocked, 'that would be
horrendous!'

They laughed, leaving the others wondering what this
was all about.

Together they walked on through the fields, the road
sometimes flanked by a row of beech trees. There were

flowers by the roadside and now and then the sun was dimmed by a passing cloud.

Barfield halted for a moment and then stated: 'This is such a very English landscape, it's unique in its scenery.'

'Indeed', Tolkien added, 'I can almost hear a few bars of Ralph Vaughan Williams' 'Pastoral Symphony'.

'Ah!' Lewis said, 'there you have a special one! Not only the music - which is very English indeed - but the character of the composer as well. I saw him one day at a concert. You know, he's the largest man I've ever seen and I understand that when he is composing he eats biscuits all the time.

He's the one who said that in every art there is ten percent of creation while the rest is hard and genuine spadework.'

Then Williams joined the discussion: 'I especially like his work when it hints on English folksongs, like some of the music of Parry and Bridge. It's a bit lighthearted, but it can be a blessing for the ear.'

Tolkien nodded and said: 'I guess it's the duty of Christian composers and writers alike to reflect in their art the image of God.'

Lewis agreed: 'That's why he probably wrote such wonderful choir music and songs inspired by religious themes.'

They had stopped walking and admired the landscape. It was Barfield who continued the conversation: 'I think that in modern English music there is a special role for the late Frederick Delius. For me he stands out from his contemporaries because of the spiritual dimension in his work.

His music sometimes has an unworldly character. They even say he had direct contact with the world of Faery and that he got some of his melodies as a gift from the elves.'

'That's certainly outstanding', Lewis said, 'did you hear that, Tollers? If anyone, you should know about this, isn't it?'

'Well', Tolkien said, 'I don't know about the elves. In my opinion elves are not usually inclined to share these things with mortals. But who knows?'

'Isn't his music just more European than English?' Williams suggested, 'with more influences of the French impressionists? As far as I know he lived in France most of his life.'

'That's true', Barfield admitted, 'and at the end of his life all inspiration must have come from within, as he was blind and paralyzed at the time.'

Turning to his companions he asked: 'you know the story of young composer Eric Fenby? Hearing of the physical condition of Delius he traveled all the way to France to help Delius write his compositions. Without Fenby there would have been no 'Songs of Farewell' or 'A Song of Summer'. And he did that for six years, till Delius passed away.'

He looked at his friends to see the impact of his words.

'Imagine, gentlemen', he continued, 'what a sacrifice that must have been. A genuine act of Christian charity, I'd say. And a heavy burden when you know that Delius was a convinced atheist.

53

Suppose Coleridge was our contemporary and we heard
he turned blind and paralyzed, would we have done the
same?'

That appeared to be a difficult question and it took some
time before the first answer came.

'No', Williams was the first to admit, 'I'd be willing to
help, but not six years of my life.'

Tolkien nodded, 'I would consider my 'New Hobbit'
just as important. Besides, I would never leave my 'little
one' for so many years.'

'And certainly not for France!' Lewis added in disgust.

They laughed and continued their route to Luxborough.

After some time, Lewis stopped for a moment to study
his map.

'I hope we're almost there', Williams said, 'I'm getting a
bit hungry.'

'And I'm longing for a beer', Tolkien added.

Lewis folded his map and said: 'patience, gentlemen' it's
almost done.'

He pointed his finger to a group of houses in the
distance. 'That's the village of Kingsbridge and that's
where we'll stop. We won't get as far as Luxborough, as
it isn't on our way.'

'What do you mean?' Williams said, 'I'd love to see the
church of St. Mary and especially the cemetery with
some very old stones.'

'I'm afraid that would be quite a detour: from here the
path goes straight on to Wheddon Cross. And as we have
to do a lot of climbing on the way, I wouldn't favor such
a visit.'

'I see', Williams said. 'Well then, let's get ourselves some
food!'

They entered the village of Kingsbridge and soon found their way to the Royal Oak pub. The name of the pub was well chosen, as all the furniture was made of oak-wood. They walked in to the courtyard and took seats at a table in the shadow of a big tree. Williams lit a cigarette and the others stuffed their pipes. Soon large puffs of smoke spiraled up to the sky.

At that moment a young woman came up to their table. With her long curling hair and blue-green eyes she looked very attractive. She held a tray in her hand and asked them in a lovely voice: ' Good morning gentlemen, what drinks can I bring you?'
'And a very good morning to you, my dear', Lewis answered, 'you really light up our day. What's your name?'
'Arwen', she said, waiting for them to order.
'Ah', Lewis reacted, 'a beautiful name for a beautiful woman.'
He saw her blushing and hastily continued to order: 'we'd like to have three beers and.....one tea I think, Williams?'
Williams nodded.
'And some bread and butter and cheese, please', Lewis added.
'Thank you, gentlemen', she said, 'I'll be back soon'.
And with these words she turned around and disappeared inside the pub.
'What a lovely creature', Williams murmured, still holding on to the vision of the girl.
'She certainly is a beauty', Barfield agreed, 'and also very elegant, as if she's of noble blood.'

'Well, maybe that's the 'royal' in the name of the pub',
Lewis suggested with a smile. 'In this region you never
know; anyone can be a descendant of Lady Guinevere.'
'I think her looks had more something of the Elvish
appearance', Tolkien said, 'I've never seen anything like
it before.'
'Then we all agree', Lewis resumed, 'that she's very
special indeed.'

When the girl returned, she ignored the way the
gentlemen were looking at her and placed the food and
drinks on the table. 'Here you are, gentlemen', she said,
cheerful as always, 'enjoy your meal!'
'Thank you, my dear', Lewis said, 'we certainly will!'
She was used to strangers acting like this, surprised by
her appearance in this local pub. The few locals in he
courtyard were more interested in their beers and game
of dice. She was, after all, one of them.
And then there was this stranger in the corner of the
courtyard, dressed like some kind of monk, who kept
looking at her from under his hood. His dark little eyes
followed her wherever she went and she was relieved to
return to the pub again.

The four Inklings enjoyed their food and
drinks. Climbing through the forest had made them
hungry and they all knew there would be more hills to
climb. In the meantime they discussed a number of very
important issues, like the weather in spring this year,
compared to the weather in spring last year. Soon they

had finished their meal and the moment the inn-keeper walked past their table they ordered some more beer.

'What happened to your lovely waitress?' Lewis asked.

The inn-keeper looked up and smiled. 'Arwen?' he said, 'oh, she has the afternoon off. Had some business to attend to.'

When he returned with the beer, they asked him if there was any news on the situation at the Czechoslovakian border.

The inn-keeper shook his head and said: 'No, not that I know of. It's been quiet for some time.'

'Well', Tolkien said, 'isn't that what they call it? Silent diplomacy?'

Williams tried to be optimistic: 'Well, I guess that's good news - I mean: as long as they're talking, they aren't fighting.'

'You mean no news is good news?', Lewis interrupted.

'I'm afraid we'll never know', Barfield said, 'so we can only hope for the best.'

They all drank to that and then stuffed another pipe.

As always it was Lewis who mentioned it was time to leave. 'We still have some climbing to do before we arrive in Wheddon Cross', he warned them.

They put on their rucksacks and paid the inn-keeper.

Outside the pub Lewis studied his map and then showed them the way. 'We have to cross the river and then walk in the direction of Lype Hill', he said, pointing his finger.

They walked down the road to the bridge, when suddenly they heard a scream.

They all stopped and looked around and then to each other. Was it a cry for help?

There was another scream, louder and more desperate then the first one.

It was a female voice.

'Quick', Barfield said, starting to run and waving his arm to invite his friends to join him.

'It's around the corner', Williams said, running right behind Barfield.

Tolkien and Lewis followed and within a minute they had rounded the building.

They were all shocked by what they saw.

It was the girl from the pub and she was not alone. She struggled to try to get away, but a strange man, dressed like a monk held his arm firmly around her neck. In his other hand he held a knife, the blade shining in the sun.

'Help!' she cried out.

The stranger tightened his grip, so that she almost couldn't breathe.

Williams took some steps forward and raised his arms.

'Please, don't hurt her', he begged, ' and for God's sake, stay calm...'

His words didn't have the desired effect. On the contrary, as the other Inklings drew closer, the stranger became more upset.

'Stay there!' he shouted, waving his knife, 'don't come any closer, or I'll kill her!'

At that moment the hood fell from his head and they saw a face that was vaguely familiar.

'Crowley!' Williams uttered, recognizing the dark magician of The Golden Dawn.

The stranger laughed and cried: 'Williams! Ah, It's you, right? You damned Rosicrucian traitor!' And then he started murmuring incomprehensible words, of which only 'Thelema' was clear enough to distinguish and repeatedly mentioned.

'What are you doing here?!' Williams almost yelled.

'Ha!' Crowley said in a sarcastic tone, 'I'm on holiday, just like you! Lovely Somerset!'

And with these words he looked at the girl who was still struggling to get free.

'Let go of her!' Barfield shouted, taking another step forward.

'Don't move!' Crowley yelled, pointing the knife in Barfield's direction.

The magician took a step backwards, but he hadn't looked where to place his foot. For a moment the root of a tree almost made him lose his balance. It was enough for the girl to escape from his grip and run for her life towards the pub.

Crowley gasped and looked bewildered at the running girl.

Then he decided that four against one - even though he had a knife - was too much of a risk.

He turned around and started running in the opposite direction. For a man of his age, he could run like the devil.

The four Inklings were too surprised to chase him. In no time the magician had disappeared behind the trees.

'Oh, my God', Williams sighed, leaning against a tree.

'That old fool!' Lewis said, angry with the whole situation.

'I'm afraid he's gone', Barfield concluded, 'but what the hell was he doing here?'

'I guess we'll never know', Tolkien answered, 'I'm just grateful that no harm was done.'

Suddenly, a deep voice behind them said: 'Gentlemen! If you please?'

They turned around and there was a policeman, standing with his arms folded for his chest.

'I heard screams', he said, a bit suspicious, 'what on earth happened?'

'Well, constable', Lewis started, 'there was this man.....'

'Please!' the policeman said, raising his hand to stop Lewis' words.

'I will have to make a report', he explained. And inviting them with his hand he said: 'would you be so kind to follow me to my office?'

He turned around and started walking down the road, expecting the Inklings to accompany him.

Being law-abiding citizens, they followed the constable back to the village.

The policeman stopped in front of a house that didn't look like an office at all. He opened the door and invited them to come in. They entered the house and followed him through the corridor to a small room with a writing desk and several chairs.

'Please, gentlemen', the policemen said, inviting them to enter the room. They all went in, looking at the furniture, the papers at the desk and the picture on the wall: it was a Somerset landscape.

As soon as they were in the room, the constable closed the door from the outside and locked it. They were too surprised to say anything at first.

'Did you hear that?' Tolkien said, 'I think he locked the door!'

Lewis tried the door-handle, but the door wouldn't open.
It was locked.
He banged on the door with his fist and shouted:
'Constable! There must be a mistake!
Can you open the door please?'
There was no reaction and they didn't hear a sound in the
corridor.
'He's gone', Lewis concluded. 'He's gone and left us here
in this room. Can you believe it?'
'Oh, my God', Williams said, 'what's wrong with this
man? You don't think he suspects us of anything, do
you?'
'I hope not', Tolkien answered, 'but for now it's the only
explanation.'
'But that's ridiculous!' Williams almost shouted.
'We know', Barfield said, 'but does the constable know?'
They fell silent for a moment. Then Lewis took two
steps to the door and threw his shoulder against it.
Nothing happened.
'The door is made of thick oak-wood', Barfield warned,
'you will only hurt yourself.'
Lewis grunted and looked around for another way out.
The room had only one window, but there were iron bars
on the outside.
'Smashing the window is no option either', Barfield
concluded.
'Then all we can do is sit and wait?' Tolkien asked.
'I'm afraid so', Lewis said, taking a chair.
The others did the same, still looking around the room.

For an hour they talked about ways to convince the
constable of their innocence. He would only have to ask

the girl in the pub; she would tell him what had happened. Or they could try to escape the moment he came back. Two of them would distract him while the others would slip away to get help.

Suddenly they heard some noise on the other side of the door. They all jumped to their feet and listened.

Someone turned a key in the lock and then opened the door.

They expected to see the constable, so it was a great surprise to them that it was the girl.

'Arwen', Tolkien said, ' How did you...?'

The girl put a finger over her mouth and whispered: 'please, gentlemen, not a sound. My father is asleep, so we have to hurry. Follow me.'

And with these words she turned around and stepped into the corridor.

'Her father...?' Williams started, but Barfield indicated he should be silent.

They followed her to the front door and then went outside.

It was a relief to be free again and feel the sun on their faces.

'How can we thank you?', Lewis said, turning to the young woman.

'No, gentlemen', she said, 'I must thank you. What's more: I owe you an apology on behalf of my father. You came to my rescue and yet you were locked in.'

She shook her head and continued: 'I'm so sorry. Since my mum died my father is very protective and he always thinks I'm in mortal danger.'

'Well', Tolkien said, 'I must say, this man was by all means a queer fellow.'

'We accept your apologies', Barfield said, in reaction to her words, 'but there's really no need. We understand and we are glad that no further harm was done.'

'Thank you, gentlemen, you are very kind.'

Then Williams stepped forward, put his right hand gently on her head and said:

'God bless you, child, under the protection'.

She blushed and thanked him with a little bow of her head.

The others weren't surprised; they were used to Williams' blessings of mostly young women.

'We'll be on our way then', Lewis said, 'we have to get to Wheddon Cross and we already lost an hour.'

'It's that way', Arwen pointed out. 'And you'd better not take the main road. I'll tell my father you went in the direction of Roadwater.'

'Good idea!' Barfield said and started walking.

Arwen raised her hand: 'I wish you a very pleasant journey, gentlemen. Or.......Elendil?'

The last words she almost whispered and only Tolkien really heard what she said.

He smiled when he passed her by, knowing that 'Elendil' means 'Elf-friend' in Old English and saw the sun radiating from behind her head. For a moment she looked like a descendant of the Vanyar, from some long forgotten age.

'Navaer', he whispered, meaning 'farewell' in the Elf-language of Sandarin and then happily continued his journey.

Much later than expected they crossed the bridge over
the Washford River. The path ahead was through
pastoral fields and over sloping hills.
'Gentlemen', Lewis started, while he kept walking, 'we
lost more than an hour of our valuable time, thanks to
this constable of Kingsbridge. Wheddon Cross is still six
miles to go, but the path it is steep and we have to climb
all the way up to Lype Hill. I suggest we only take a rest
at the top of the hill and then continue till we arrive in
Wheddon Cross.'
'Agreed', Barfield answered, walking right behind Lewis.
The others nodded their heads in consent.

From there the path went uphill for almost three miles,
so they had to save their breath for the climb. The
weather was nice that day but they were glad with
the scattered clouds that sometimes blocked the
sunshine.
Every now and then they stopped to take a sip from their
water-flask. In spite of the effort it took to climb,
Williams started talking to Tolkien who walked next to
him.
'This girl Arwen was very special, don't you think?'
'O yes,' Tolkien agreed, 'she was very special indeed!'
'If Coleridge had met her, I'm sure it would have inspired
him to write beautiful poetry, in the same way that
Beatrice did to Dante.'
'I'm sure he would. She had the beauty and youth to
inspire people, but for me there was more: her
appearance reminded me of an angelican or Elf-like
being from a long-lost age.'

'Really? It sounds like she's inspired you too.' He smiled understandingly and then continued: 'I just hope she's safe. Who knows where this devil Crowley has gone? It was an evil moment when this man crossed our path.' Tolkien nodded his head. 'That man brings evil wherever he goes; I hope we'll never see him again.' After these words they fell silent for some time, concentrating on the path uphill.

Around them they saw the sloping hills with the green and yellow fields. Every now and then they spotted a small farm and in the distance they noticed woodlands. They had reached Colly Hill, which was the next step to Lype Hill, but still the path went up. 'Come on, gentlemen', Lewis encouraged them, 'some more climbing and then we can start the descent to Wheddon Cross.' They sighed and followed Lewis uphill, longing for a rest at the top. The top of Lype Hill rewarded them with a magnificent view of the Brendon Hills, a range of hills from West Somerset to the East of Exmoor. They took the time to catch their breath and enjoy the view. 'Why would anyone call this Lype Hill?' Williams wondered. 'Well, I don't know about that', Tolkien said, 'but what I do know is, that this hill used to be called Brunedun, in Old English it means 'Brown Hill'.' 'Right', Lewis said, 'Then I suggest we leave the brown hill for the brown ale of Wheddon Cross.' He pointed with his finger in the distance: 'it must be somewhere over there. From now on it's downhill all the way, gentlemen, so let's get going!'.

Together they started the descent to Wheddon Cross, sometimes correcting Lewis because he marched too briskly, leaving the three of them behind.

'You know', Barfield said, 'that farmer we spoke yesterday, was right after all. There were strange creatures on the road. Just think of it: the friendly English countryside and then this Crowley, coming from another world.'

'It's always possible', Lewis reacted, 'as this is a planet of good and evil, of dark forces and forces of light. In 'Out of the silent planet' I tried to make a comparison between Earth, ruled by corrupted fallen angels and a 'pure' planet Mars, still without evil and ruled by Beings of Light.'

'You mean angels or archangels?'

'Yes, exactly, although I don't use the word 'angels'. They have another kind of existence; they live and work more closely to the Creator of everything and they are less material then we are.'

'I see', Barfield said, 'which means you can only describe their existence in terms of vibrations, like in the worldview of Goethe and Steiner.'

'That's right. For Beings of Light to come into our world it's the same as for us to go under water. You enter another world, with other conditions and sensory perceptions.'

They stopped for a moment and waited for Tolkien and Williams to join them.

'Well Jack', Tolkien said, 'I'm ready for a beer. How far is it?'

'We're getting close', Lewis answered, 'it's not very far from here.'

And to cheer them up he said: 'You know, my brother
Warnie once said that his idea of a happy life would be
to buy a pub and then put on a notice: 'NO BEER'.'
They all laughed at the idea and continued on the last
part of the descent.
At the end of the afternoon they at last entered the
village of Wheddon Cross. Soon they found their way to
the 'Rest and Be Thankful' Inn. 'What's in a name',
Tolkien said, upon entering the pub. They found a table
and dropped into the chairs to give their poor legs a rest.
And then they ordered beer. Lots of beer.

5

THE ROAD TO PORLOCK

Wheddon Cross, May 1938

After a good night's rest they had breakfast together the next morning. The mood was mixed, as today would be the last part of their walking tour. 'Well, gentlemen', Lewis started, a teacup at hand, 'the weather today is good for walking: a few clouds and not too warm. We will start walking in the direction of Dunkery Hill - the highest point in Exmoor and Somerset.' He waited a moment and after the first sigh from Williams he continued: 'But don't worry, we won't have to climb it.' He smiled and sipped his tea.

'That's good', Williams reacted, 'I'm glad we won't have to'.

'On the other hand', Lewis continued, 'we'll be walking through moorland and some forests, sometimes up- and sometimes downhill.'

'That's not so good', Williams said, although it wasn't clear whether he meant the climbing or the forests or both.

'Well, I'm fine, Tolkien said, 'and I can't wait to continue our tour'.

'Just a moment', Barfield said. He had been talking to the inn-keeper and now returned to their table. 'You won't believe this', he said mysteriously. 'Remember the statements from London and Paris about the German troops at the Czechoslovakian border?'

They all nodded and waited for Barfield to continue.

'Well, it turns out the whole story was some kind of a hoax: there are no extra German troops at the border, so all the excitement was for nothing.'

'Really?' Williams uttered, rather surprised.

'That's strange', Lewis said, 'I wonder who fabricated that story in the first place.'

'Maybe the Germans', Tolkien said, 'to see how we would react in a situation like that.'

'Smart thinking!' Barfield laughed, complimenting his travel companion, 'and now that they know our reaction, they will probably think twice to actually maneuver their troops.'

Tolkien shook his head. 'I doubt it, gentlemen. There's a dark shadow rising in the East and Evil is growing there.'

'Please, Tolkien', Williams interrupted, 'Don't spoil our last day. I'm relieved to hear it was just a story and I hope Barfield is right.'

'Well, let's all hope for the best', Lewis concluded, 'Shall we, gentlemen?'

And with these words he pointed towards the rucksacks, standing near the door. They all got up, said farewell to the inn-keeper and left the building with their rucksacks on their backs. On the outskirts of the village they followed the road sign to Dunkery Hill. After some time they passed Raleigh Manor, a beautiful country house that used to be part of the estate of sir Walter Raleigh.

The path now went uphill through some woodland. But before Williams could mutter something about trees and forests they entered an open field where they had to cross a small stream.

'Some more woodland to go', Lewis announced, pointing at the trees in the distance, 'Blagdon Wood, in fact. But after that there will be only moorland, when we will be walking around Dunkery Hill.'

'Glad to hear that', Williams said, 'I'd like to see Dunkery Hill, but with all these trees there's no real view yet.'

'Just wait and see', Lewis answered, 'You will see enough of the hill; enough to get bored and thirsty, as there's no pub in the surroundings'.

'Well', Barfield reacted, 'that is what I call a problem.'

'So do I', Lewis admitted, 'I hope we can stop somewhere in Luccombe. It's not very far from the road to Porlock'.

Tolkien turned to Lewis and said: 'I trust your love and instinct for beer. Surely you will find us the right place!'

Lewis smiled and put a hand on Tolkien's shoulder. 'You know, Tollers, there once was a time that I thought Roman Catholics and Philologists could not be trusted.' He laughed and continued: 'But since I know you - you are both a Roman Catholic and a Philologist, after all - I understand it's nonsense to think like that!'

Tolkien laughed as well and said: 'Then at least that's something I accomplished!'
Now they all laughed. After that they were silent until they reached the first trees of Blagdon Wood.

It was an old forest. The trees were large and majestic and with their long branches they seemed to protect the next generation of woodland. The younger trees and the lower scrub together formed thick walls of twigs and leaves, sometimes making the path look more like a green tunnel. They walked down hill, next to a stream that on Lewis' map was indicated as the River Avill. Walking in the forest each Inkling undoubtedly had his own images coming to mind at that moment. Maybe Tolkien was thinking of Forest Elves or big spiders, populating the woodlands of The New Hobbit, Lewis perhaps of the more quiet parts of Narnia and Williams of the enchanted forest of Broceliande, at the end of the world near the Atlantic coast.
'I love these woods', Tolkien started, 'And I have loved trees all my life. They are a great inspiration to me.' He looked around, still walking, and continued: 'And I also love the hills of Somerset. But what I do miss, are the mountains.'
'The mountains?' Williams asked, not understanding, 'There are no mountains here.'
'I know, I know', Tolkien answered, 'But high mountains and deep valleys always make a more dramatic scenery. I'm sure I will incorporate them in The New Hobbit.'
'Ah, I see', Williams said. 'Talking about The New Hobbit; do you read it to your son Christopher? I know he liked the first hobbit story.'

71

'Oh no!', Tolkien answered, almost shocked, 'I certainly don't! You see, The New Hobbit is not a bedtime story like the first Hobbit was. And Christopher is only twelve. If I told him about The Black Riders he probably wouldn't sleep for five nights. I couldn't do that.'
'I understand', Williams said, 'I just hope you will share your adventure with us when you read us the next chapter on Thursday evening.'
'I will, but probably not next Thursday, because I can't write while I'm walking'.
Williams smiled and nodded his head.

They carried on walking slowly downhill through the forest. Twice they had to cross a side stream of the river Avill. Lewis attempted to put Williams at ease, but the way he tried wasn't very successful.
'Don't worry, Williams', Lewis said, 'this forest isn't very wide, we'll reach the last row of trees before you know it. This is nothing compared to Horner Wood where we'll be walking this afternoon. That's a lot bigger.'
Williams didn't look very happy with this perspective. Lewis tried again: 'But halfway through the forest we'll take a break and find some place in Luccombe where we can have a beer. Or some tea', he added.
Williams still looked a bit worrisome, but he thanked Lewis for his effort.
After a few hundred yards the path went up again and they reached the end of the forest. The last part of the climb was steep, but on top of the hill they entered the open moorland of Dunkery. In the distance they saw the massive height of Dunkery Hill, rising against the horizon.

Having left the forest behind, Williams was more at ease and started talking.

'For me this walking tour is special, because it is almost the same route that was taken by Taliessin, the poet at the court of King Arthur.'

'Is that so?' Lewis asked.

'Yes, as a young man Taliessin traveled South, along the West Coast of England to Wales, in the direction of the magical forest of Broceliande.'

'And?' Lewis asked, a bit impatient, 'why did he go there? It doesn't sound like a pleasant destination.'

'No, that's true', Williams admitted, 'but it was more like a kind of pilgrimage. In the forest of Broceliande all things come together: in a secret part of the forest lies Carbonek, the mythical Castle of the Holy Grail. And that's another legendary goal to reach for, even if you never attain it. For the search for The Grail is a noble mission in itself.' And then, almost apologetically: 'It's all very symbolic, of course.'

'Of course', Lewis affirmed, 'but as far as legends are concerned, the stories of Arthur and his Knights of the Round Table are the best we have in Britain.'

'Quite right', Williams continued, 'and therefore I'm working on a long poem about Arthur and what he stood for. The poet Taliessin is the most appropriate vehicle to tell the story, because it's the poets who make these stories into legends.'

'That sounds very interesting, Williams', Tolkien intervened, 'so you tell the stories of Arthur from the point of view of this poet?'

'Yes, but it's more than that. For me Arthur is a symbol of Hope, the King who not only unites all of Britain, but who stands for the whole of Western Civilization. His Round Table is based on noble principles like co-inherence, substitution and courtly love. Merlin, The Grail, the Lady of the Lake, they're all part of this mythical tapestry that is doomed to vanish in the mists of time.'

Lewis knows why: 'Because Arthur dies on the battlefield'.

'Right', Williams continued, 'At the battle of Camlann, where all evil forces unite, Arthur dies by the sword of Mordred, the traitor. Arthur is then taken to the Isle of Avalon by Taliessin and Britain sinks back in a pre-Roman chaos of tribal wars and dissension.'

'That's the real drama', Barfield said.

'Well', Tolkien added, 'Is it any different these days? There's evil growing in the East. How long will it take before we'll be at war again?'

'Come on, Tollers', Lewis said, 'Let's not be too pessimistic. Maybe we actually learned something from Sarajevo.'

'I pray we did', Tolkien answered, 'but I sometimes doubt the learning skills of Man'.

They strolled on, meanwhile enjoying the wide view of the moorlands. The sun was shining, there were a few clouds and there was a little breeze, that made perfect conditions for walking. They kept Dunkery Hill to their left and followed the path in the direction of Brockwell. Barfield walked next to Williams and picked up on the previous discussion.

'I guess the way you make Taliessin revive the tales of Arthur is most of all a matter of metaphor, isn't it?'

'Well, yes', Williams answered, 'that's certainly true. Arthur and his Round Table symbolize the best and most civilized part of Mankind and the Quest for the Holy Grail is in essence a metaphor for the spiritual path.' Barfield nodded and said: 'You see, I've been studying this for some years now; did you know that metaphor in itself is an indicator for civilization?'

'What do you mean?'

'Well, if we go back in time - and I mean a very long way back, when we as a species first began to look like humans - we started to give names to things and animals around us. Before that we were one with nature and we experienced the world quite differently.'

'You mean these humanoids at first did not distinguish between us and them?'

'Yes, that's right. It was the act of giving names to things and animals in the outside world that made us distinguish between us and the rest of the world in the first place. Too many researchers imagined prehistoric Man from our modern world perspective, but that is altogether wrong. They didn't experience the world as we do. A number of researchers even presupposed they were stupid, but that's not the point. They were less analytic and more part of a group; they had a totally different mindset.'

'Not as individual as ours', Williams said.

'Yes, quite, that's the point! But when they started giving names, that was the first moment they distinguished between themselves and the outside world. Their language was, of course, very direct and specific. Branches were sticks - things that you could use to build a home or hit an enemy. When we talk about the

branches of an organization, they wouldn't understand what we are talking about.'
'That's more abstract.'
'Yes and that's where metaphor comes in. Language develops with civilization, and the more distance we create between ourselves and the reality outside, the more we create meaning in an abstract sense. Sometimes a word has different meanings, depending on the context. Take the Latin word *Spiritus* which can be translated as *breath* as well as *wind*. But the next step is that it becomes a metaphor for *Spirit* or that elusive medium that gives life to Man and Animal alike.'
'Interesting', Tolkien said, joining his friends.
'Our modern language is full of metaphors', Barfield continued, 'but we don't really recognize them as such. When you say 'I don't have the stomach for that', you may literally throw up at the idea of killing someone, but usually it has a psychological meaning. The same goes for many other metaphors with parts of our bodies, like heart, liver, feet, eyes, back, etc. So what is really interesting is the moment a metaphor is born or used for the first time. That's the moment when a metaphor is most powerful - it gives new meaning to an already known word or concept. Coleridge was very good at it. As far as I know he was the first to use the metaphor of the *Point of View*.'
Barfield smiled and saw Lewis also joining them. 'But the real metaphor-maker was of course Shakespeare. Using metaphors for the words of his characters have made his plays very dynamic and powerful. Shakespeare called 'sleep' the *balm of hurt minds*. In his play King John, Lord Salisbury - hearing of the death of young

Arthur - says: the *ruin* of sweet life. The metaphor '*ruin*' is very well known to us, but in those days it must have been strange to hear it for the first time.'

Lewis nodded his head and said: 'I suppose the real challenge was to create new metaphors that were fresh and strange, but still comprehensible.'

'That's right', Barfield answered, 'a metaphor that no one understands misses its effect. But when a metaphor becomes part of everyday language, it loses its power as well.'

'Like shadows rising in the East?' Lewis asked, jokingly.

'Come on, Jack', Tolkien reacted, a bit irritated, 'that's still a powerful metaphor and you know it!'

'All right, all right', Lewis said, his hands raised as if he was blessing someone.

They had come to a halt, while discussing the history of metaphor. Lewis looked around, studied his map and then said: 'Well thank you, professor Barfield, for your most interesting lecture on metaphor. Maybe one day we can discuss this a bit further, but for now we have to continue our journey.'

And then to all of them: 'gentlemen, follow me!'

With these words he started the descend into Hanny Combe, at the bottom of which they had to cross another stream. After that the path went uphill again.

When the direction on the signs changed from Brockwell to Webber's Post, Williams called for Lewis, who was walking up front. 'Jack', he said, 'can't we stop in Brockwell? We are very close now and I'm getting a bit thirsty.'

Barfield agreed: 'I'd love to have a beer.'

'Well', Lewis said, 'I would like a beer too, but as I already said, I planned to stop in Luccombe. That way we will be halfway through the forest and we a lot closer to Porlock'.

'Okay', Williams sighed, 'we'll do it as planned.'

And with Lewis leading the way they walked uphill in the direction of Webber's Post and beyond that the wide contours of Horner Wood.

Around lunchtime they entered the forest, not far from Webber's Post. It was to be a short visit, because they had to leave the path pretty soon to get to Luccombe. After a few hundred yards Lewis changed to another path to the right and before they knew it they were out of the woods. Before them they saw green meadows, farmland, rows of trees and a number of farms and houses.

Near Luccombe they passed the old tower of the Church of the Blessed Virgin Mary. Williams had no time to search his big book for a reference on the church, because everyone was too thirsty and wanted to carry on. At the end of the street the turned left and found themselves in the yard of an old manor house. Lewis turned around to his companions and said: 'As there is no pub in Luccombe, I hope for the hospitality of the people who live here.'

He was not disappointed. The landlord walked onto the courtyard with open arms, greeting his visitors and inviting them to take a seat at the table outside. He waved to a maid to bring food and drinks and within ten minutes they were all enjoying the local beer. It was a blessing for their dry throats and they were happy to tell the landlord for where they had come from and where they were heading.

'Well, that's quite a walk', the landlord said, 'all the way through the Quantocks. So Porlock will be the end of the road for you?'

'Yes', Lewis confirmed, 'from there we return to Oxford, so we can have some sleep in college.'

They all laughed at this remark and drank their beer.

After having eaten some bread and cheese and smoking their pipes they were ready to pick up their trail.

They thanked the landlord for his hospitality and took on their rucksacks.

'I wish you a good journey', the landlord said, 'for you gentlemen there's only the forest left to cross.'

Lewis looked at him and asked: 'That can't be too hard, can it?'

'Well, that depends. Parts of the forest are very, very old. Some of the oaks there go back in time more than 500 years. They say the forest has a memory of its own.'

'So?'

'Well, I don't know, but one hears all kinds of stories.'

Lewis didn't like the way the conversation had developed, knowing that Williams wasn't very fond of woodlands, to say the least.

'What kind of stories?' he asked.

The landlord shrugged and said: 'Sometimes people return from the forest frightened to death. Only they can't report what happened.'

At that moment he saw Williams turn pale and immediately he tried to put them at ease: 'but there are four of you gentlemen and you don't look very superstitious to me, so I suppose everything should be all right.'

He raised his hand: 'Well, good luck then.'

'Yes, thank you', Lewis said and started walking from the courtyard.

The others followed him and within a few minutes they had left Luccombe in the direction of Horner Wood.

When they entered the forest they could sense a different atmosphere. It was hard to say if that was because of the words of the landlord, but it just *felt* different.

Horner Wood certainly was an old forest. The trees were massive and their branches long. Most trees were oaks, but there were also ash trees and rowans. On the ground there were large groups of ferns and there were lichens growing against the trunks of many trees.

Tolkien knew that Horner Wood was famous for its many different types of bats, but wisely didn't mention it. Bats, after all, wouldn't be around until twilight. And by that time they would already be in Porlock.

'Haven't seen a tiger yet', Lewis said, jokingly.

'Oh, come on, Jack', Tolkien reacted, 'Let's not play that game again.'

'All right, all right; I admit: the chance of meeting a tiger is almost nil, but who knows? Maybe the forest will surprise us.'

They walked on for a few hundred yards and nobody said a word. All they could hear were their own footsteps on the forest path and sometimes the rushing of leaves or the cracking of branches.

Lewis didn't feel at ease, but he did his best not to show it and certainly not to say it. He had the feeling they were being followed and with each step that feeling grew stronger. He looked around, but couldn't see a sign of anything strange.

Suddenly Barfield stopped, turned around and raised his hand: 'Gentlemen, I think we're being followed. I hear more footsteps than just ours and it is coming from over there.' He pointed to some bushes on the right side of their path.

They had all stopped now and listened intently for sounds of someone drawing near. But all they heard was the wind blowing through the leaves.

Barfield shook his head. 'I'm sure I heard something.' They walked on, their attention now focused more on the bushes than on the path.

'There!' Barfield shouted, pointing again to the right, 'can you see it?'

They all peered into the bushes, noticing movement.

'Maybe it's a deer?' Lewis tried.

'No', Tolkien said, 'a deer wouldn't be following us.'

'It's that damned Crowley again!' Williams shouted, picking up a branch to defend himself.

Tolkien did the same and at that moment they also detected movement in the bushes on the left side of the road.

'There are more of them!' Williams yelled, looking scared and not knowing what to do.

'Stay calm, Williams', Lewis said, 'Let's stick together, with our backs against each other. That way we can face the enemy!'

They formed a little circle in the middle of the path, each armed with a stick.

There was more stirring in the bushes and Williams shouted: 'Come on, Crowley, you miserable creep! Come out and show yourself!'

At that moment a man stepped out of the bushes onto the path. He was armed with a pistol and had a helmet on. Two others followed, both armed with rifles. On the other side of the path three more soldiers appeared, with helmets and rifles.

'I'm terribly sorry, gentlemen', the first one said, putting away his pistol, 'Did we frighten you?'

'Well', Lewis said in a loud voice, 'what does it look like?'

His companions lowered their sticks as they were no match for the rifles of their opponents.

'As I said', the first man, probably an officer, repeated, 'I'm terribly sorry sir, but you are in the middle of a military exercise. Didn't you see the signs on the road?'

'No we did not', Lewis answered, still a bit irritated, 'when we walk we don't take the road, but mostly hiking trails and bridleways.'

'Ah, I see. And you are heading for Horner?'

'Yes, Horner and then Porlock. Does this mean we can ran into another ambush every single mile?'

'Oh, no', the officer said, 'They won't get as far as us, so you'll be all right if you follow this path.'

He stepped forward and held out his hand.

'Lieutenant Bowman, sir, Somerset Light Infantry.'

Lewis shook his hand and said 'Lewis, lieutenant, and these are my friends.'

'Pleasure, gentlemen', the lieutenant said, tipping his hand against his helmet.

'Lieutenant', Williams asked, 'do you think there's going to be a war?'

'Ah', the lieutenant answered, 'that's not for me to say, sir, I'm afraid. That's up to the politicians.'

'Well then', Tolkien murmured, 'Let's hope then they'll do better than in 1914.'

'Let's certainly hope so', the lieutenant said, waving to his men to follow him.

They bid one another farewell and the soldiers disappeared into the bushes.

For a moment the four Inklings looked at each other. Then they started laughing.

'Well', Lewis said, 'that wasn't a deer and it wasn't Crowley either.'

'I'm glad it wasn't', Williams reacted, 'I wouldn't like to see his face again'.

'And I'm glad to see that our army is doing some training', Tolkien said, 'who knows how much we'll be needing that.'

That started walking again, as usual with Lewis leading the way.

They reached Horner without any more disturbances. Lewis refused to look for a pub, as it was but a small village and Porlock wasn't far away. 'It's better to continue' was his statement.

After passing Horner Mill, they crossed the river over the late medieval packhorse bridge, also known as the Hacketty Way Bridge.

'The end of our journey is near', Lewis said, studying his map. 'From here we walk on the edge of the woodland,

with the river on our right side. We'll soon be in
Porlock.'

They carried on a bit faster, as they were all looking
forward to a glass of beer as a reward for all their pains.
'Do you think these soldiers were 'men from Porlock?'
Tolkien asked.

'Well', Lewis answered, 'I doubt it. At least they were not
the men who disturbed Coleridge when he was working
on Kubla Khan'.

And then he continued: 'By the way, Williams, is there
anything on Porlock in your big black book?'

'Yes, indeed', Williams said, 'I looked it up earlier.
There's an old church, partly 13th century, that is
dedicated to the saintly Celtic Dubricius. According to
legend, he was the one who once crowned King Arthur.'

'Ah!' Lewis smiled, 'then we're still on Taliessin's trail,
right?'

Williams smiled upon hearing the poet's name. 'It sure
looks like it.'

Near Porlock the path went up again, but they all knew it
would be for the last time. They reached the first houses
of the village and soon found the street leading up to
Porlock Hill. Once on top of the hill they had a splendid
view of the Bristol Channel.

'At last', Tolkien said, 'the end of our journey'.

'Indeed', Barfield agreed, 'and quite a journey it was.'

With these words they entered the old 'Ship Inn' to order
some beer and smoke their pipes.

6

HOMEWARD BOUND

In Transit, May 1938

Next morning they had a good breakfast at the Ship Inn.
It would be their last for some time on the Somerset
coast. Outside it was a bit more cloudier than the day
before, but there was no rain and visibility was still
good. They packed their belongings and enjoyed the
view once more, before starting the journey home.
'I love these views of coastlines and oceans as far as the
eye can see', Tolkien confessed. 'You can imagine all
kinds of ships sailing along these coasts; Drake and
Nelson's warships of the line, or centuries earlier the
smaller ones used during the Viking-raids.'
'Or the imaginary Elven vessels', Barfield suggested,' on
their way to Eressea, or the warships of Numenor
heading for the coast.'

Tolkien smiled; Barfield had a good memory. 'True', he said to Barfield, 'with some imagination you can even see the Island of Numenor in the distance, as if it had never been destroyed.'

'I wonder', Barfield said, 'if the myth of Atlantis had not been such an integral part of western mythology, would the story of the Fall of Numenor have been as strong and impressive as it is now?'

'I'm afraid not', Tolkien said. 'But in essence the drama is always the same: whether you call it Atlantis or Numenor or the biblical story of Sodom and Gomorrah: it's all about the arrogance of Man and the vengeance of the Gods.'

Williams joined them and said: 'Then I hope the Heavens will intervene when mister Hitler has the arrogance to conquer the whole civilized world.'

'I hope so too', Barfield agreed, 'but to be fair: till now these interventions only happen in stories. Where were the heavens on the battlefields of the Somme?'

At that moment Lewis waved at them to head for the road. It was time to go.

They traveled by local bus from Porlock to Taunton. During the first part of the ride the bus used the coastal road, with lovely views of the Bristol Channel, but from Watchett it went south, straight to Taunton railway station. As the last part of the road ran close to the Quantock Hills, it brought all kinds of memories of the first days of their walking tour.

In Taunton they boarded the train to London; later in Reading Tolkien and Lewis would change trains for Oxford.

It was a pleasant journey; the English landscape unfolded before their eyes, while the train ran through the hills of Wiltshire.

At that moment all four Inklings had their own mixed feelings. They looked back at a wonderful walking tour and at the same time looked forward to the obligations of the coming week.

'I must say', Williams started, 'that I'm very glad I don't have to walk this day'.

Barfield smiled: 'I couldn't agree more, Williams. I believe four days is just about the limit for me.' And to the others: 'You see, in London City you don't get much walking practice.'

'That's true', Lewis said, 'you two really kept up very well. Tollers and I do get more of a chance to walk in the surroundings of Oxford.'

'And there won't be much of a rest', Tolkien warned, 'for tomorrow it's back to work again!'

They all nodded and some sighed. But Lewis reminded them: 'Tomorrow is Tuesday, remember, so in the morning I'll be at the Bird & Baby.'

'So will I', Tolkien said, 'but I doubt that our companions will find the time to come.'

'I'm afraid not', Barfield said, 'I've a lot to do in London.'

'Same goes for me', Williams added, 'tomorrow it's back to the pile of manuscripts.'

They all laughed at this image of Williams' desk.

'Speaking of manuscripts', Lewis said, looking at Tolkien, 'I always hope that one day you will pick up the story of 'The Lost Road' again. Will you read a new chapter next Thursday?'

'No', Tolkien said, 'I'm afraid that case is closed for now. At the moment I'm working hard on The New Hobbit and I don't have time for anything else.'

'That's a pity', Lewis concluded, 'after all, I kept my part of the bargain: last month I published 'Out of the Silent Planet.'

'Bargain?' Barfield asked, 'what kind of bargain?'

'Well', Lewis started to explain, 'Tollers and I both like the science fiction genre and a few years ago we were thinking it would be an interesting challenge for each of us to write a science fiction novel. That was more or less the bargain: I would write a novel on space travel and that became 'Out of the Silent Planet'.

And Tollers would write about time travel and that would be 'The Lost Road'.

'Only I didn't finish it', Tolkien interrupted, 'it was indeed a 'lost road'.

'I still think it's a very interesting theme', Barfield said, 'I loved reading 'The Time Machine' by H.G. Wells.'

'Ah yes, it's a great theme', Williams agreed, 'if we had such a machine at our disposal, I'd love to travel to 14th century Italy, to meet Dante Alighieri.'

'And I would try my luck in 18th century Germany, to see if could meet Goethe.'

'I'm afraid that would be quite an undertaking', Lewis said. 'For what I know of Wells' time machine, it all would have depended on where it was located. If that was, for instance, in London, you would have ended up in 14th or 18th century London. And from there you would have had to find your way to Italy or Germany - IF', and Lewis stressed the word, 'IF you would find yourself in the right circles, where they would have had the means for travel. But mind you: you could just as well have ended up in the gutter or in a dark part of London where there would have been only poverty, famine and disease.'

'All right, Lewis', Barfield sighed, 'You just managed to talk me out of it. What a pity - it was such a nice daydream.'

Williams also looked a bit disappointed. To get from London to Italy using 14th century transport would be quite a challenge, not to think of wars or the plague. And then there was also the sometimes doubtful precision of the time machine. A small deviation of the timeline and you could end up decennia earlier or later. He turned to Tolkien: 'By the way, did you use a machine in the concept of 'The Lost Road?'

Tolkien shook his head. 'No, I didn't like the use of a machine. Instead I used a kind of clairvoyance - time travel in the mind, so to say. That way my characters didn't have to materialize in another time or place, but at the same time they were able to experience and be witness to historical events from the first hand. Besides that, some characters also had lucid dreams, in which they were witness to historical or even future events. That's how I made a connection between 'The Lost Road' and 'The Fall of Numenor'.

'You mean your characters had nightmares about the Fall of Atlantis?' Barfield asked.

'Yes', Tolkien answered, 'at least that was supposed to be one part of the story.'

'Well', Williams spoke, 'I do hope you will find the time to finish the story one day. It sounds quite interesting to me.'

'I'm afraid I have to disappoint you on that, for I won't finish 'The Lost Road'. I'm not satisfied with the structure of the plot and the development of the story. On the other hand, I may use some elements of 'The Lost Road' in a new attempt at writing a novel on time travel.'

'What do you mean?'

'When we were on our way to Porlock and especially standing on Porlock Hill, I got this new idea for a plot.'

'Fascinating. Can you tell us a bit about it?'

Tolkien hesitated for a moment, but then agreed to share some of his ideas.

'It's all very premature, of course.'

'Of course', Williams said.

'Well', Tolkien started, 'The main characters are all part of a club of some kind, maybe something like The Inklings.'

'You mean we are going to be part of your story?' Lewis asked.

'No, not really. I mean, I'll create a few characters of my own, of course.'

'And then?' Williams asked, 'what happens?'

'I think I might use the same means of time travel as in 'The Lost Road' - time travel in the mind, lucid dreams - but with quite a different setting. The idea is, that the story unfolds when someone is reading the reports of that club; the notes they made during the gatherings. There they tell each other about their lucid dreams and the way they connect to - for instance - the Fall of Numenor close to our Atlantic coast.'

'But is it realistic', Lewis asked, 'to base your story on reports of this club? I mean, we don't make any notes ourselves, not on Thursdays and certainly not on Tuesdays. I hardly even mention them in my letters or my diary.'

'Well, I think that's a matter of poetic license; in that fictional club of mine they just happen to make notes and they do write reports. Besides: did I ask you whether you think the spaceship to Mars in your science fiction novel is a realistic way of transport?'

'Alright, alright', Lewis conceded, 'have it your way; I just can't wait to hear you read the story to us.'

Tolkien smiled. 'I will, one day, you can be sure of that. I will also keep my part of the bargain.'

Lewis also smiled, 'There's really no hurry, Tollers. And as you know I have some more science fiction to do.'

'I know', Tolkien answered, 'You're aiming for a trilogy, aren't you?'

'Yes, but the nice thing about science fiction is, that it's all in the future, so you will always have time.'

They all laughed at this remark.

Outside the landscape was changing. There were more houses now and there was more traffic on the road.

'I think the train is approaching Reading', Lewis said and then turning to Tolkien, 'so we'll have to get off soon now.'

'Ah yes', Tolkien responded, getting up and picking up his rucksack, 'it's always a pity to split up a company after so many hours of walking together.'

'True', Barfield agreed, 'And I must say it was a real pleasure walking with the three of you.'

'Indeed', Lewis added, 'and what an adventure it was! We certainly had it all: rain and shine, hills and valleys, forests and moors, lovely creatures and very weird creatures, and of course lots of beer!'

They laughed and shook hands, while the train entered the Reading railway station.

'The only thing missing', Tolkien said, 'was of course the dragon.'

'Well', Williams said, 'You just might be mistaken about that.'

'What do you mean?'

'We walked in the Quantocks and in Exmoor, but it was all still Somerset, right?

Just the other day I found out what the Coat of Arms of Somerset looks like. Guess what? It's a big red dragon!'

'So...'

'So we've been walking all these hours in de the county of the dragon!'

'Wonderful!' Lewis interrupted, 'but we really have to get off this train now.'

They said goodbye to Barfield and Williams and moved from their compartment to the doors of the train. Tolkien murmured that it would be quite some time before they would see them again. 'It's a pity, for this company of Inklings is very precious to me....'

They hadn't seen the person in the compartment next to theirs. He followed them with his eyes when they were leaving the train. This time he didn't look like a monk, but more like a tourist, with his khaki jacket, his straw hat and his sunglasses.

'Precious....'he lisped, looking at the compartment of the Inklings that stayed on the train.

From the platform Lewis and Tolkien waved to their
companions when the train left the station. Then they set
off to look for the next train to Oxford.

7

NOTES

This booklet is a work of fiction. And although it is based on numerous facts and documents, it brings together a lot of things, that may have been different in reality. In these notes I mention some of these differences.

Chapter 1.

In the first chapter Tolkien *walks* to the pub. Normally he would travel by bike, so he would be home in time for lunch with his wife and children.

The quotation '*he's reducing our walking tour to some kind of Sunday stroll*' is from Warnie Lewis, Jack's brother.

The presence of Owen Barfield in the pub is remarkable. The moment he started working in London he could no longer be present at the gatherings of the Inklings.

The presence of Charles Williams is even more remarkable. He became a member of The Inklings no sooner than in 1939, when the Oxford University Press moved its offices from London to Oxford.
In 1937 three Inklings (Tolkien, Lewis and Barfield) had already had an '*exhausting walking holiday*' in the Quantock Hills. (Timeline of the Tolkien Society). Oddly enough, this holiday is not mentioned in diaries, letters or biographies. So we don't know what route they took and what had made it 'exhausting'.

Chapter 2.
Lewis had very strict ideas on walking tours (use of the word 'hiking' was forbidden): use rucksacks, bring no provisions, visit as much pubs as possible and keep on walking, no matter the weather.
Lewis had his own vocabulary. A 'Place to Soak' meant a nice place to rest and to relax. 'Coalbiters' was the name of their literary society before they took on the name of the Inklings.
The rumour of a concentration of German troops near the Czechoslovakian border and the political turmoil it created is mentioned in history-books as 'The May-incident' or 'The Sudeten Crisis'.
Lewis and Tolkien had both been in the trenches in WWI.
Barfield studied the world view of Coleridge and would later write a book about it.

Chapter 3.
All four Inklings are known as 'Christian writers or poets'. But in their spiritual development there's more than just Christian Theology.
Lewis was a convinced agnostic, who later joined the Church of England. Barfield also joined the Anglican Church, but at the same time remained an anthroposophist. Tolkien was a Roman Catholic all his life and Williams first joined a Temple that separated from the Order of the Golden Dawn and later joined the Rosicrucians.

Chapter 4.
'Taliessin through Logres' (The Descent of the Dove) was published in 1939, but Williams was no doubt already writing parts of it in 1938.
Williams was a great admirer of Dante. Dante's writings on Beatrice were an inspiration for Williams 'Romantic Theology'.

Chapter 5.
The 'Sudeten crisis' in May 1938 led to the Munich Pact between England, France and Nazi-Germany, on the last day of September 1938. In this Pact London and Paris agreed with a German annexation of the Sudetenland, a part of Czechoslovakia. The next day the Nazi's annexed Sudetenland. In March 1939 they invaded the rest of Czechoslovakia.
The moors of Exmoor and the Somerset coast were indeed used for military training, although not earlier than in the 1940's. Tanks landed on the beaches and artillery was used on the moors.

Chapter 6.

Tolkien wrote parts of 'The Lost Road' already in 1936. In 1945 he started writing 'The Notion Club Papers' with partly the same ingredients of 'The Lost Road', only in a different setting. The papers are found in the beginning of the 21st century and they refer to gatherings in the 1980's. Prominent in the reports are lucid dreams about the Fall of Numenor, in which the village of Porlock is mentioned several times. It was Tolkien's second attempt at a science fiction novel on space travel, but he didn't finish either of them.

Of the gatherings of The Inklings on Thursdays, there are no notes or reports; moreover: none of the Inklings mentions anything about it in their letters or diaries. So when Humphrey Carpenter wrote is biography of The inklings, he added a *fictional* chapter about the Thursday evenings; hoping to give the readers an idea of how it may have been.

8

LITERATURE

Barfield, Owen, *Poetic Diction; a Study in Meaning*, Faber & Gwyer, 1928.

Barfield, Owen, *What Coleridge Thought,* Oxford University Press, 1972.

Beer, John (Ed.), *Samuel Taylor Coleridge,* Orion Books, 1996.

Carpenter, Humphrey, *J.R.R. Tolkien*, Allen & Unwin, 1977.

Carpenter, Humphrey, *The Inklings, C.S. Lewis, J.R.R. Tolkien, Charles Williams and their friends*, Allen & Unwin, 1978.

Carpenter, Humphrey (Ed.), *The Letters of J.R.R. Tolkien,* Allen & Unwin 1981.

Conan Doyle, Arthur, *The coming of the fairies*, Hodder & Stoughton, 1922.

Duriez, Colin, *J.R.R. Tolkien and C.S. Lewis; the story of a friendship*, HiddenSpring, 2003.

Fenby, Eric, *Delius as I knew him,* G.Bell & Sons, 1936.

Hooper, Walter, *Letters of C.S. Lewis, with a Memoir of W.H. Lewis*, Harvest, 1966.

Howe, Ellic, *The Magicians of the Golden Dawn; a Documentary History of a Magical Order 1887-1923*, Routledge & Kegan, 1972.
Kilby, Clyde S. (Ed.), *Brothers and Friends; the Diaries of Major Warren Hamilton Lewis*, Harper & Row, 1982.
Knight, Gareth, *The Magical World of the Inklings*, Element Books Ltd, 1990.
Lachman, Gary, *Aleister Crowley; magick, rock and roll and the wickedest man in the world*, Penguin, 2014.
Larrington, Carolyne, *The Norse Myths; a Guide to the Gods and Heroes*, Thames & Hudson, 2017.
Mee, Arthur (Ed.), *Somerset, County of Romantic Splendour*, Hodder & Stoughton, 1940.
Poe, Harry Lee, *The Inklings of Oxford*, Zondervan, 2009.
Tolkien, J.R.R., *The Hobbit*, Allen & Unwin, 1937.
Tolkien, J.R.R., *The Lord of the Rings Trilogy*, Allen & Unwin, 1954-1955.
Tolkien, J.R.R., *The Tolkien Reader*, Random House, 1966.
Tolkien, J.R.R., *The Silmarillion*, Allen & Unwin, 1977.
Tolkien, J.R.R., *Sauron defeated; the History of The Lord of the Rings, part 4 (* including *The Notion Club Papers)* , HarperCollins, 1992.
Wells, H.G, *The Time Machine*, Heinemann, 1895.

ABOUT THE AUTHOR

Kees M. Paling (1954) is a writer of several books in the
Dutch language:

- *De Wereld als Halve Waarheid (The World as Half-
Truth), 1990;*
- *Galgemaal voor Pruisen (The Fall of Prussia and the
life of Paul von Lettow-Vorbeck, general, guerrillero
and putchist), 1995;*
- *Het Fin-de-Siecle als uitdaging (The Fin-de-Siecle as a
challenge; culture on the eve of the New Millennium),
1996;*
- *Mijnheer Van Dale en de Apocalyps (Mr. Van Dale
and the Apocalypse; The End of the World in 80 days),
1999;*
- *Als je kind een leerprobleem heeft (when your child has
a learning problem), 2004;*
- *Canongebulder (Cannon Roar; what everyone should
know about Dutch Military History), 2006;*
- *Operatie Tango (Operation Tango; the Orange Coup
on Veteran's Day), 2007.*

He contributed to several books on communication, the
millennium and what if-history and was co-editor of *'The
European Challenge'*. Furthermore he wrote about 1.000
articles in daily newspapers and weekly magazines about
many different subjects.

He was educated as a sociologist at Utrecht University and fulfilled his military service as a lieutenant/student counsellor at the Dutch Royal Military Academy. He worked for 10 years at the Ministry of Culture and another 10 years at the Netherlands Institute for Social Research. Since the beginning of the new Millennium he has been working as a communication consultant for the Dutch Government.